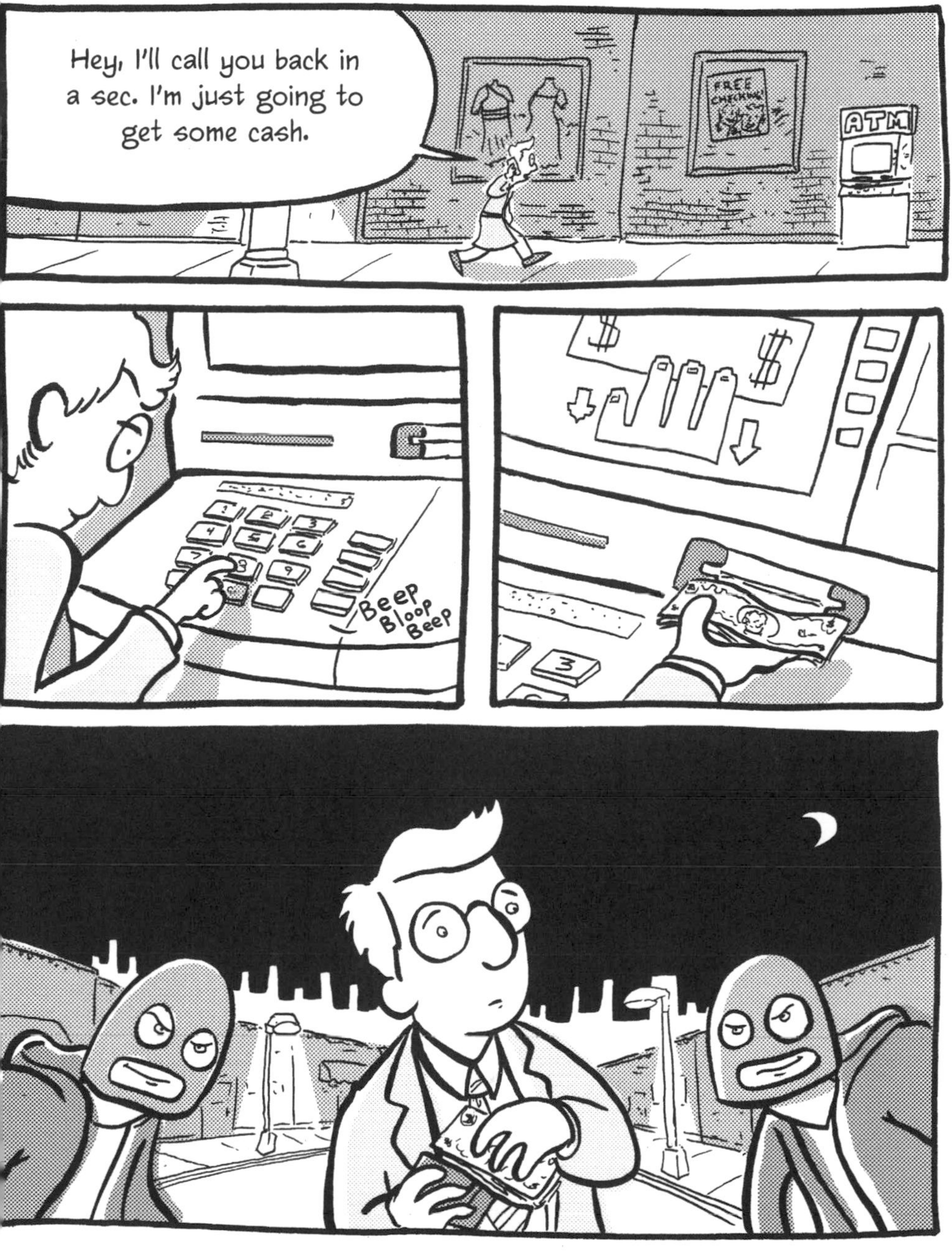
Hey, I'll call you back in a sec. I'm just going to get some cash.
ATM
Beep Bloop Beep

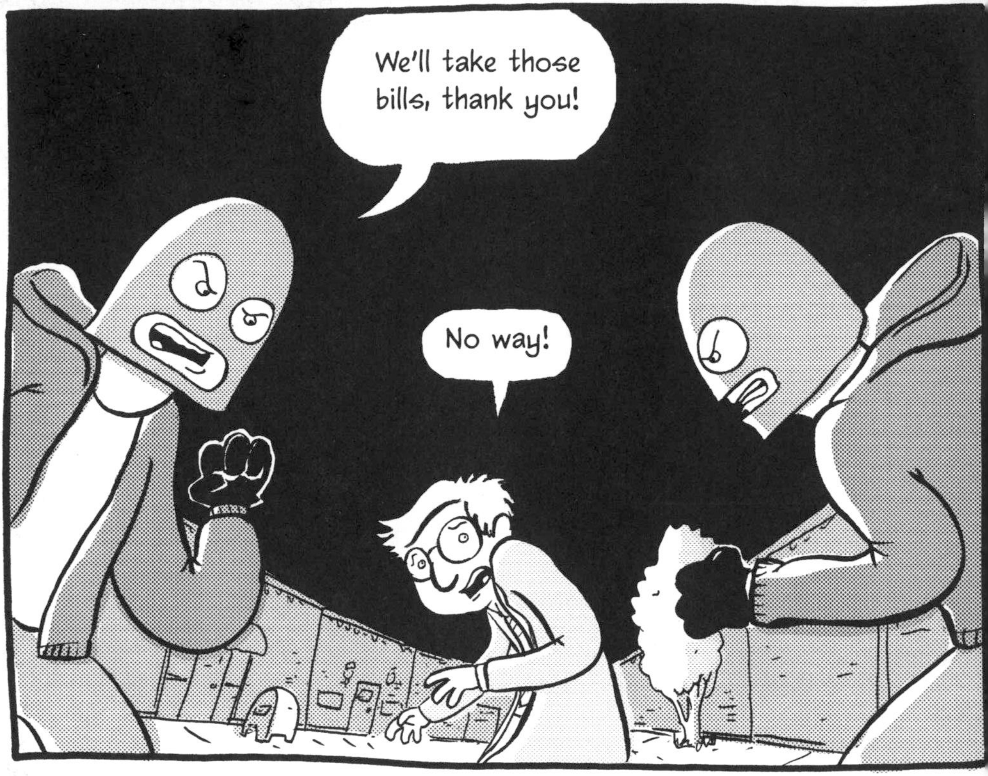
We'll take those bills, thank you!
No way!

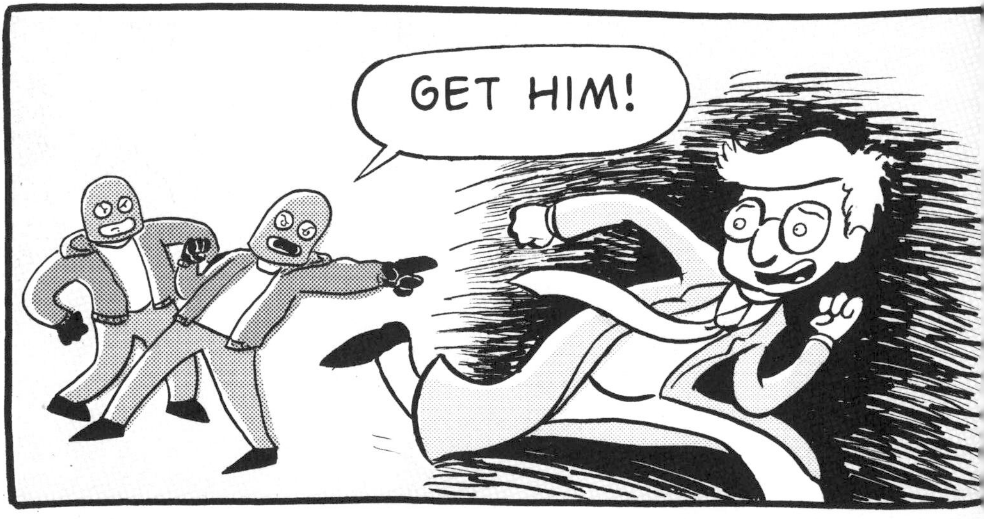
GET HIM!

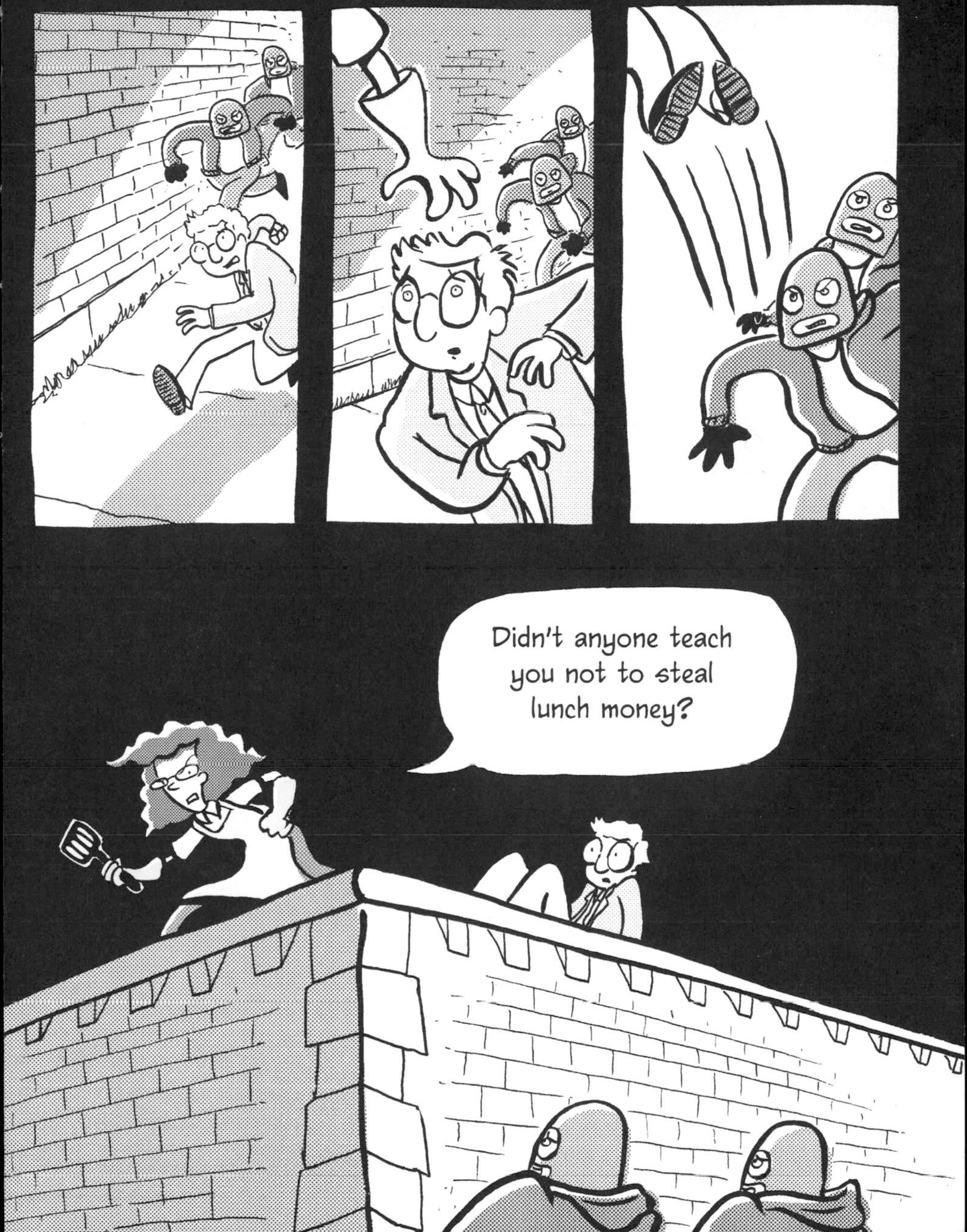
Didn't anyone teach you not to steal lunch money?

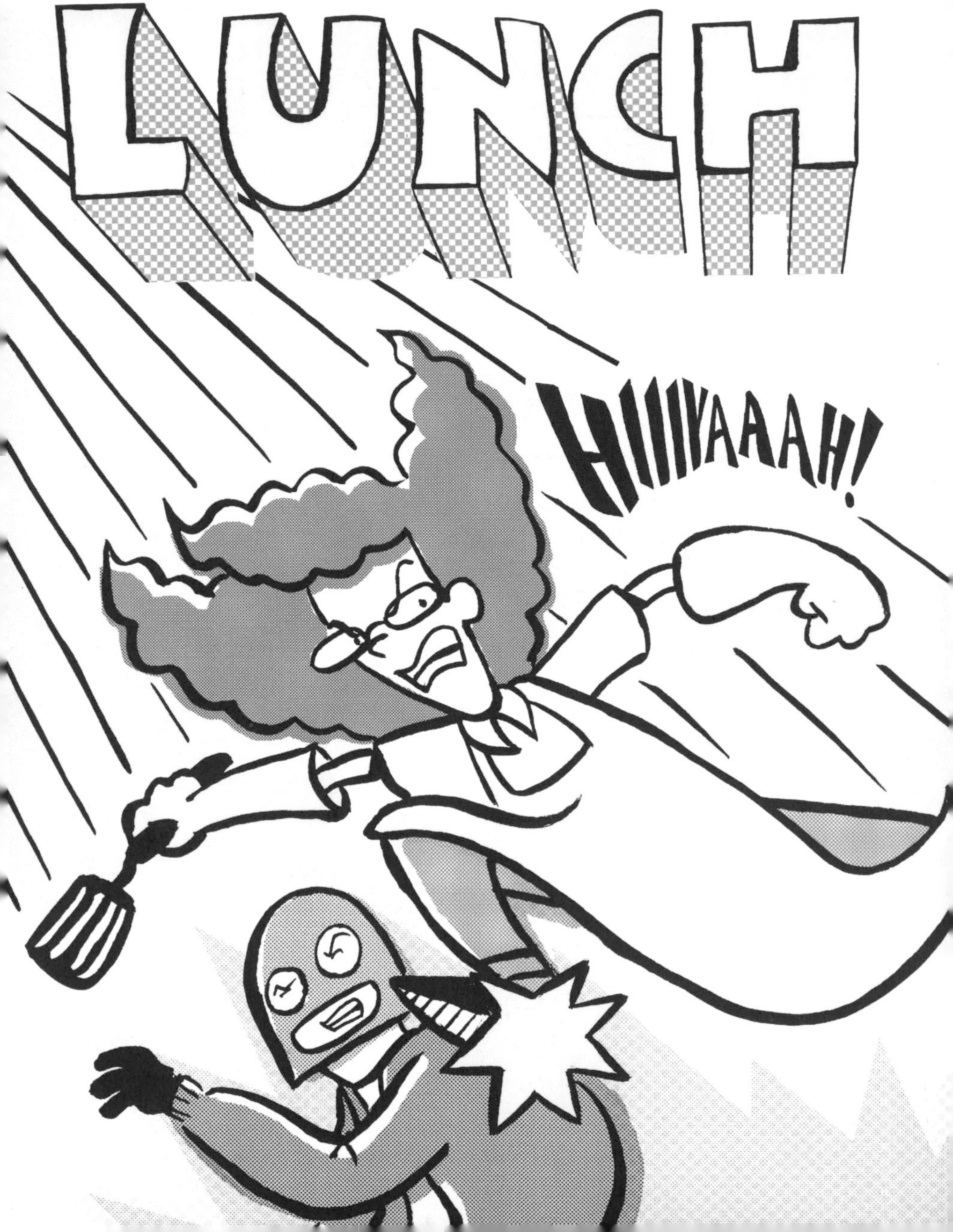
LUNCH
HIIIIYAAAH!

LADY

and the Picture Day Peril

Jarrett J. Krosoczka

Alfred A. Knopf New York

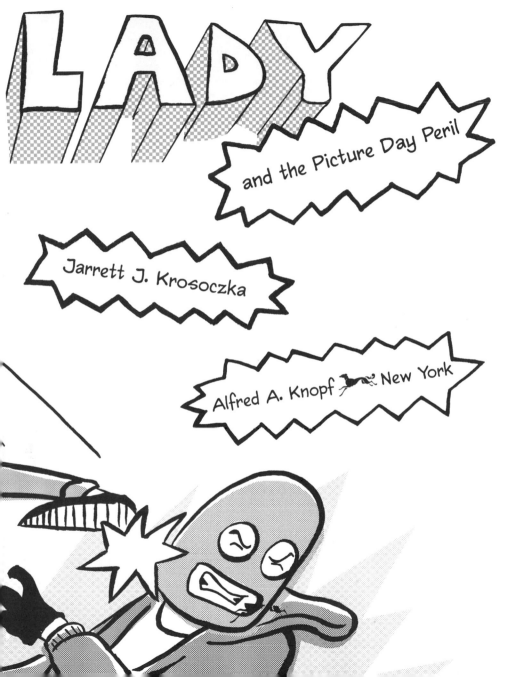

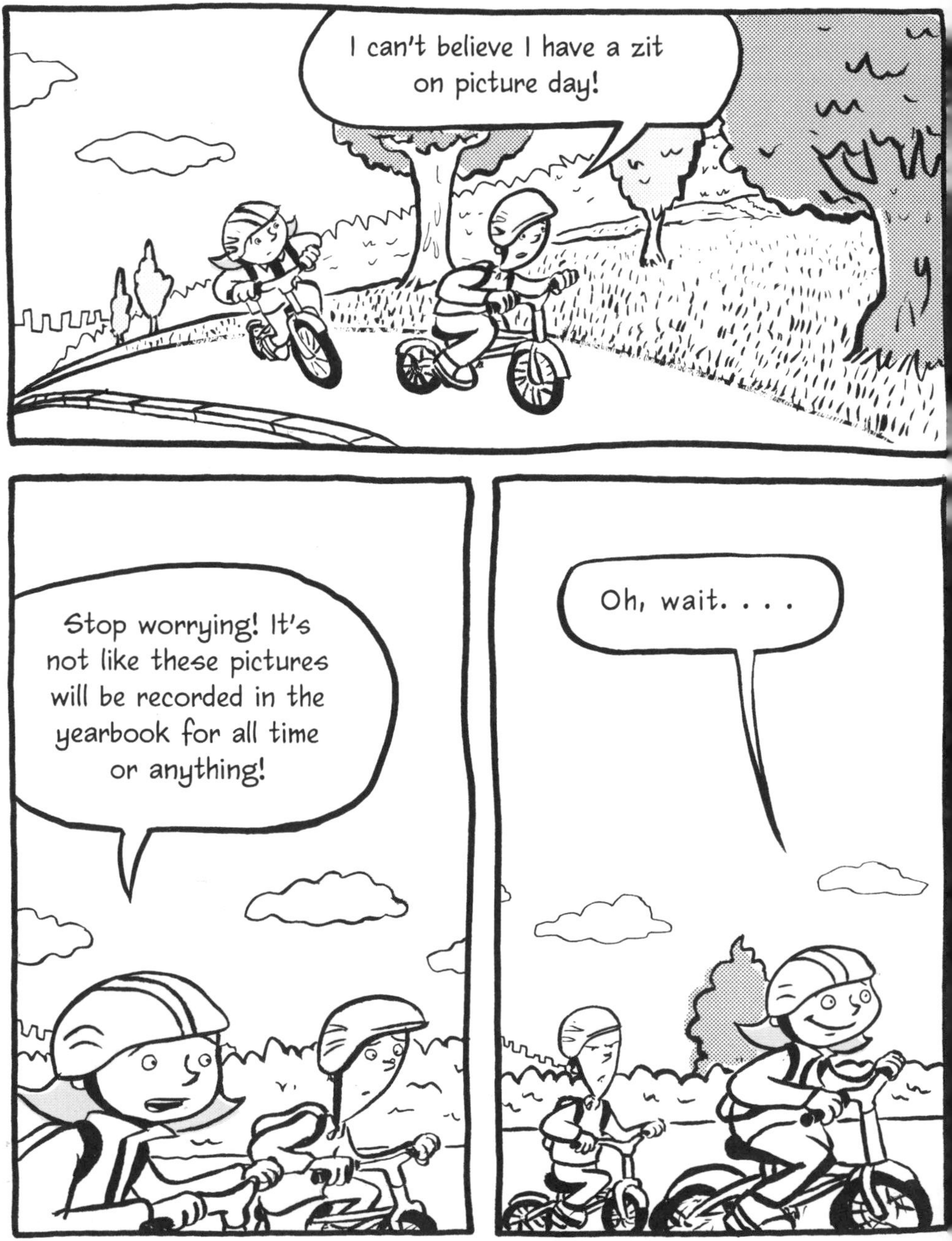
I can't believe I have a zit on picture day!
Stop worrying! It's not like these pictures will be recorded in the yearbook for all time or anything!
Oh, wait. . . .

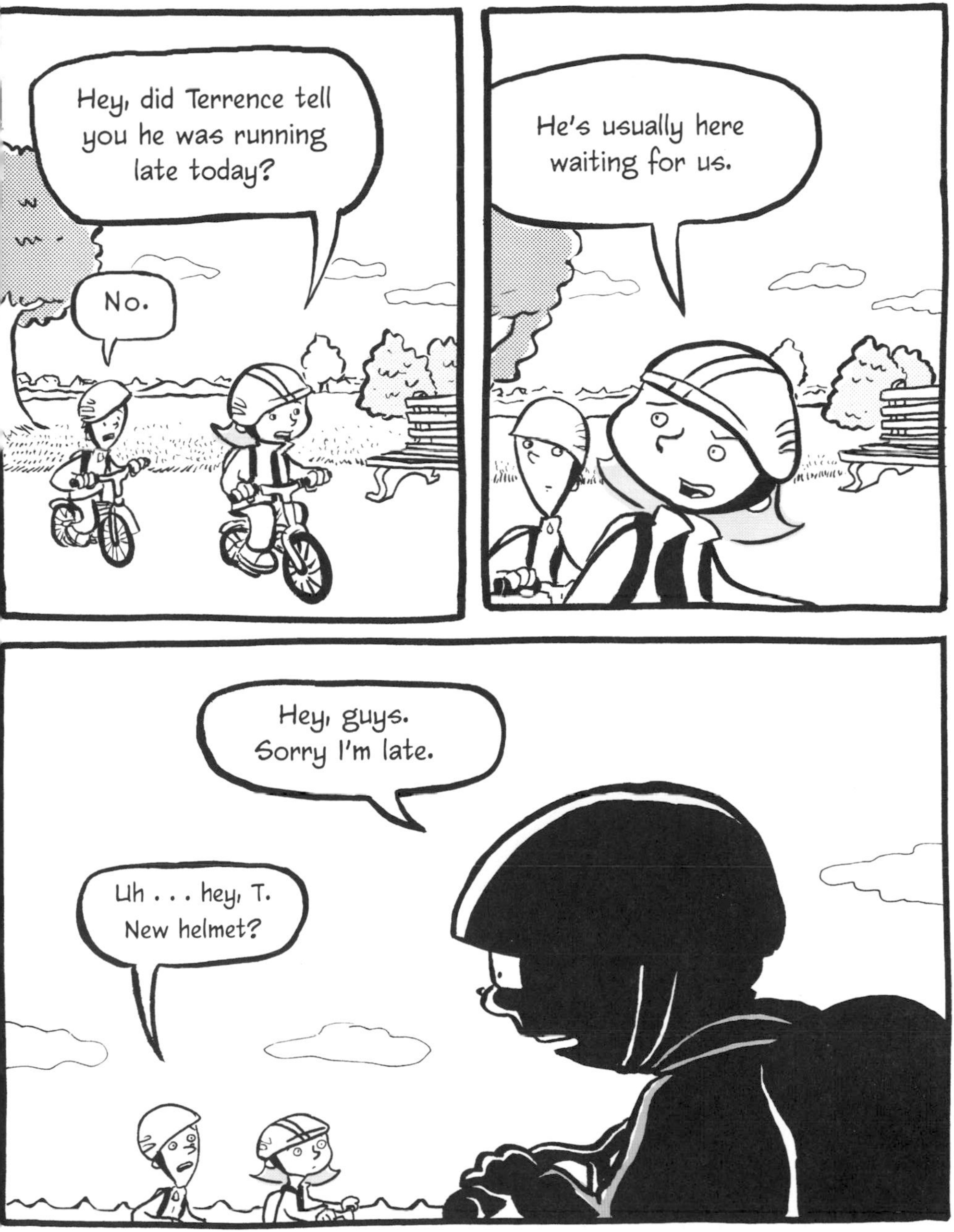
Hey, did Terrence tell you he was running late today?
No.
He's usually here waiting for us.
Hey, guys. Sorry I'm late.
Uh . . . hey, T. New helmet?

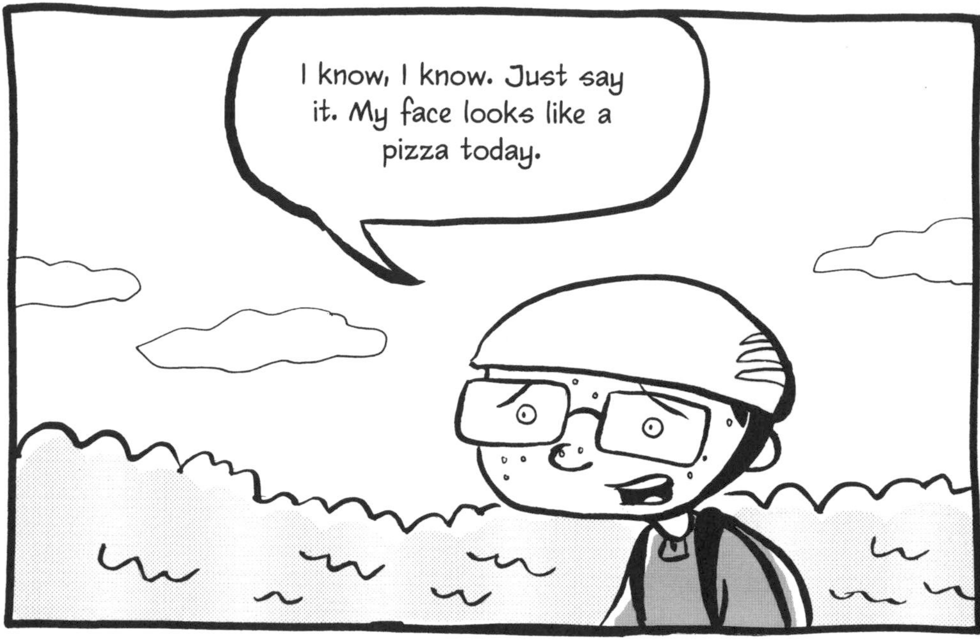
I know, I know. Just say it. My face looks like a pizza today.

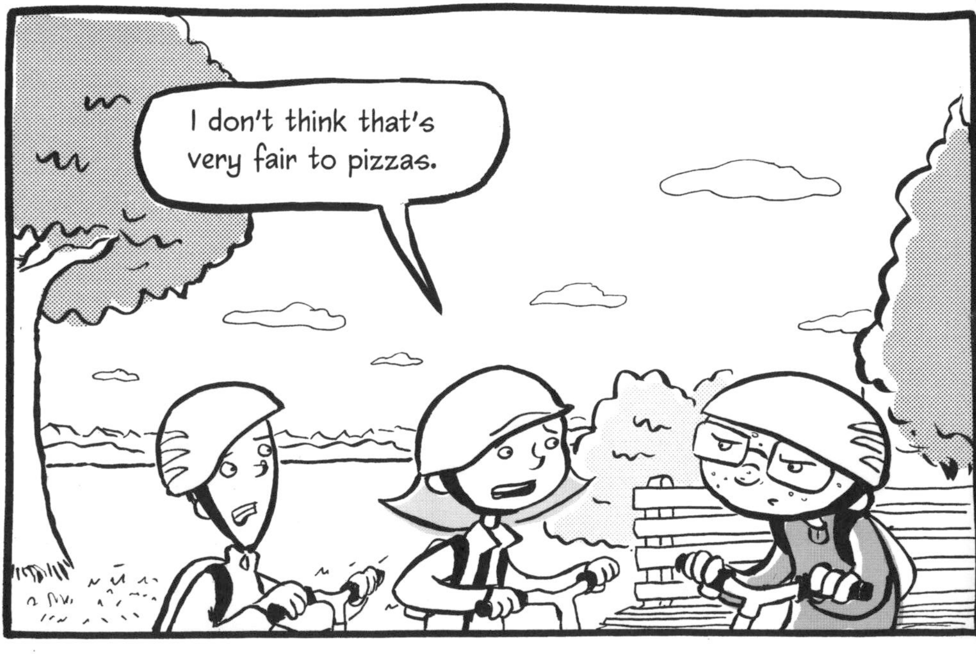
I don't think that's very fair to pizzas.

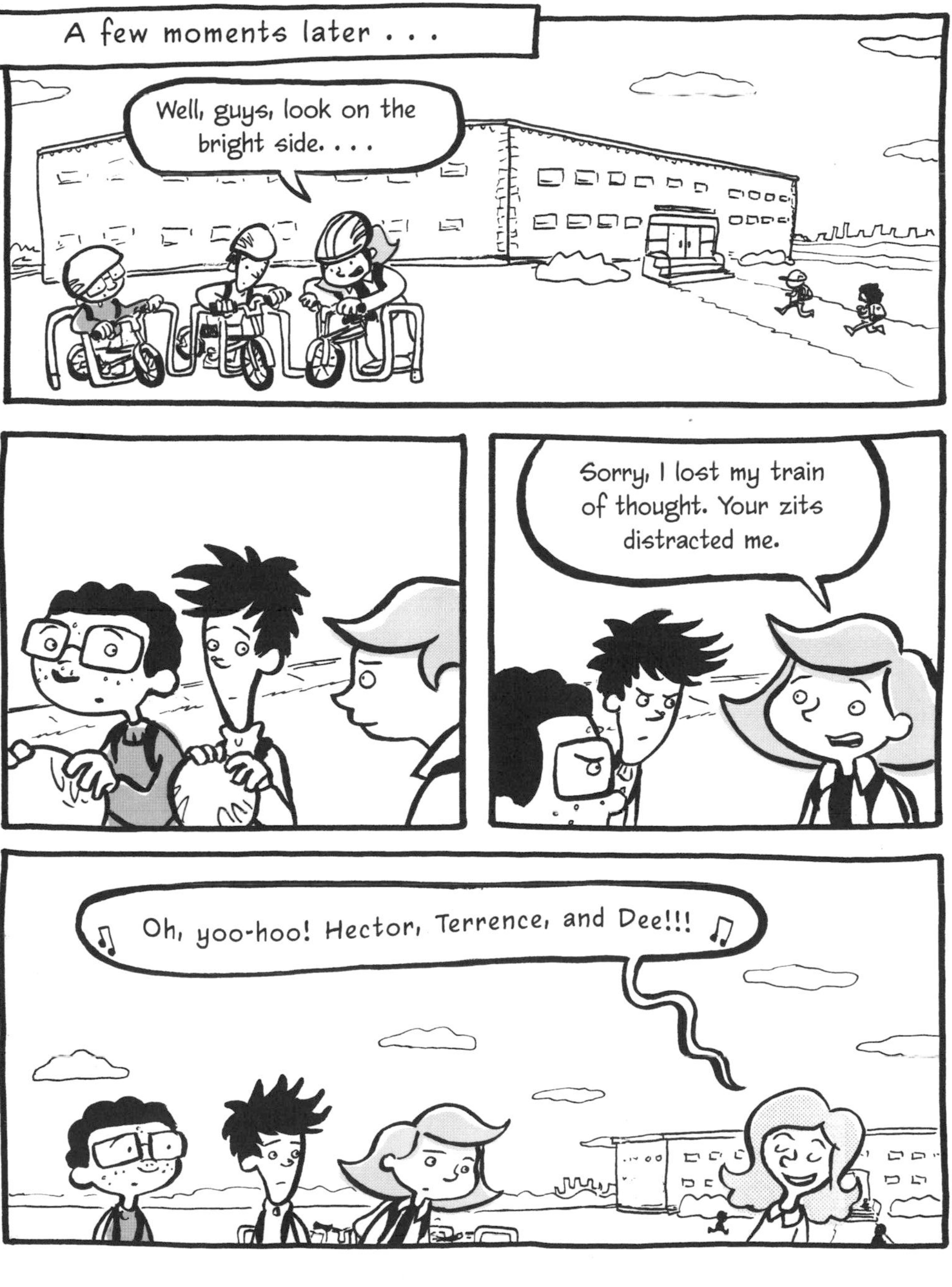
A few moments later . . .
Well, guys, look on the bright side. . . .
Sorry, I lost my train of thought. Your zits distracted me.
♫ Oh, yoo-hoo! Hector, Terrence, and Dee!!! ♫

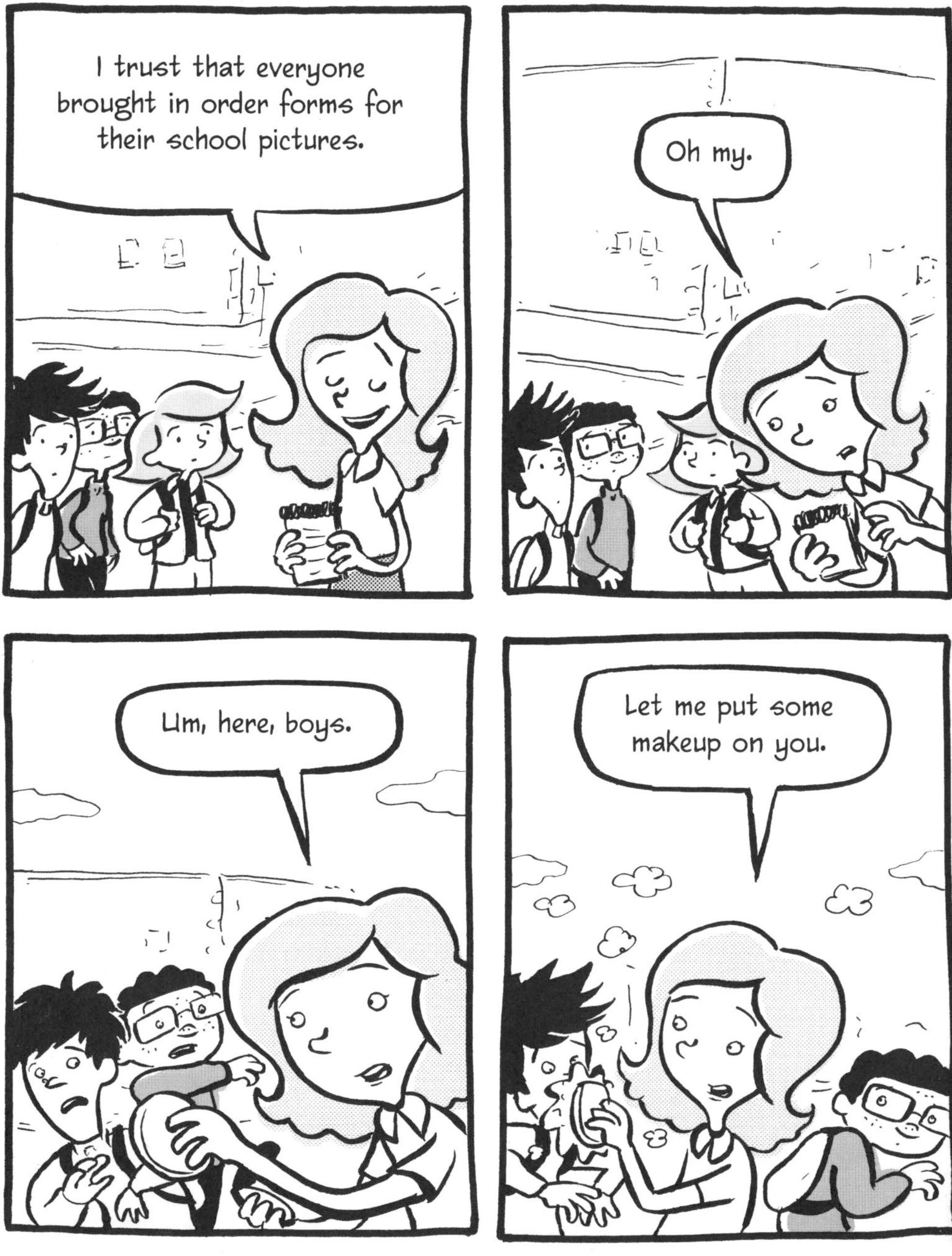
I trust that everyone brought in order forms for their school pictures.
Oh my.
Um, here, boys.
Let me put some makeup on you.

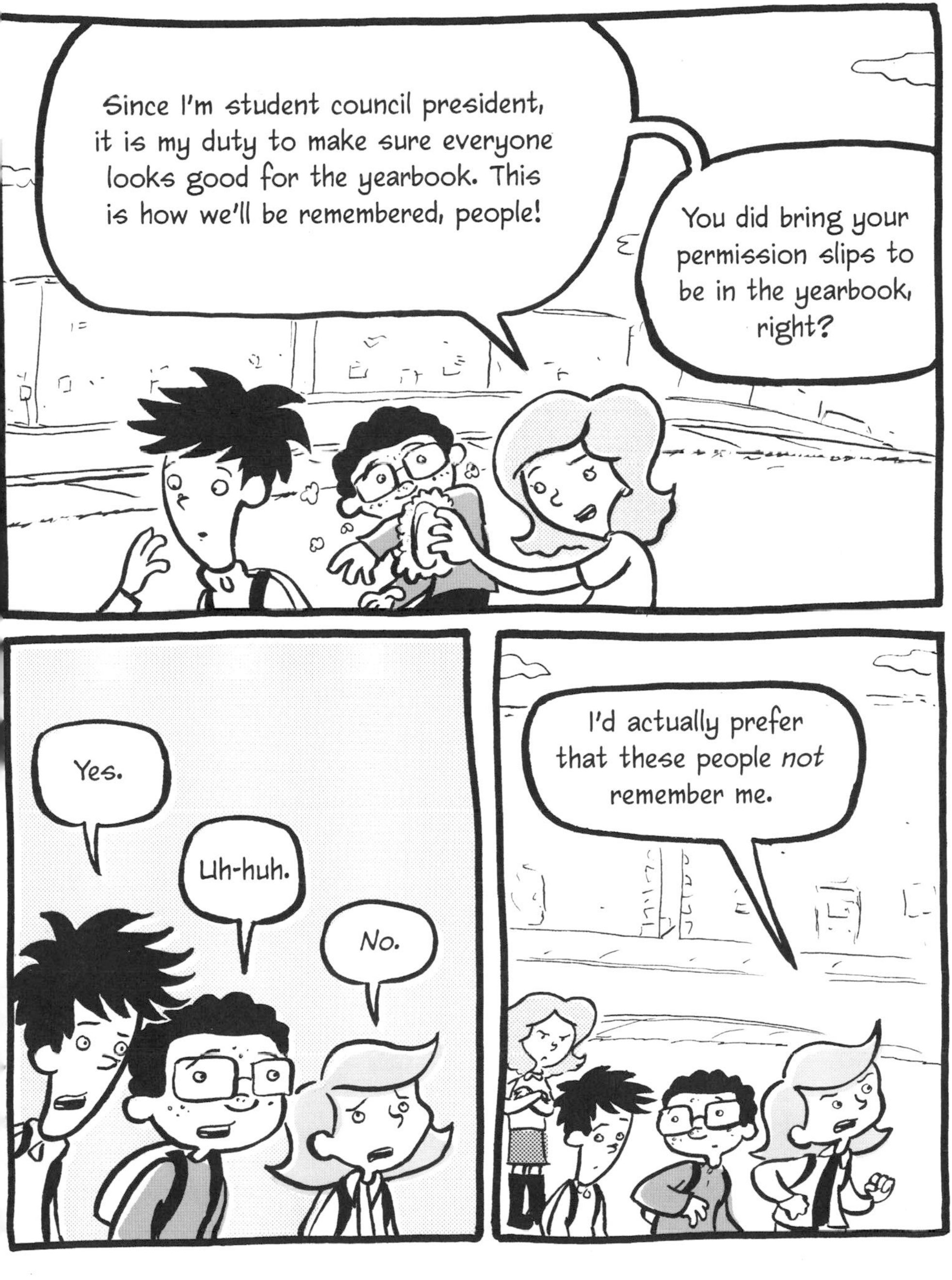
Since I'm student council president, it is my duty to make sure everyone looks good for the yearbook. This is how we'll be remembered, people!
You did bring your permission slips to be in the yearbook, right?
Yes.
Uh-huh.
No.
I'd actually prefer that these people *not* remember me.

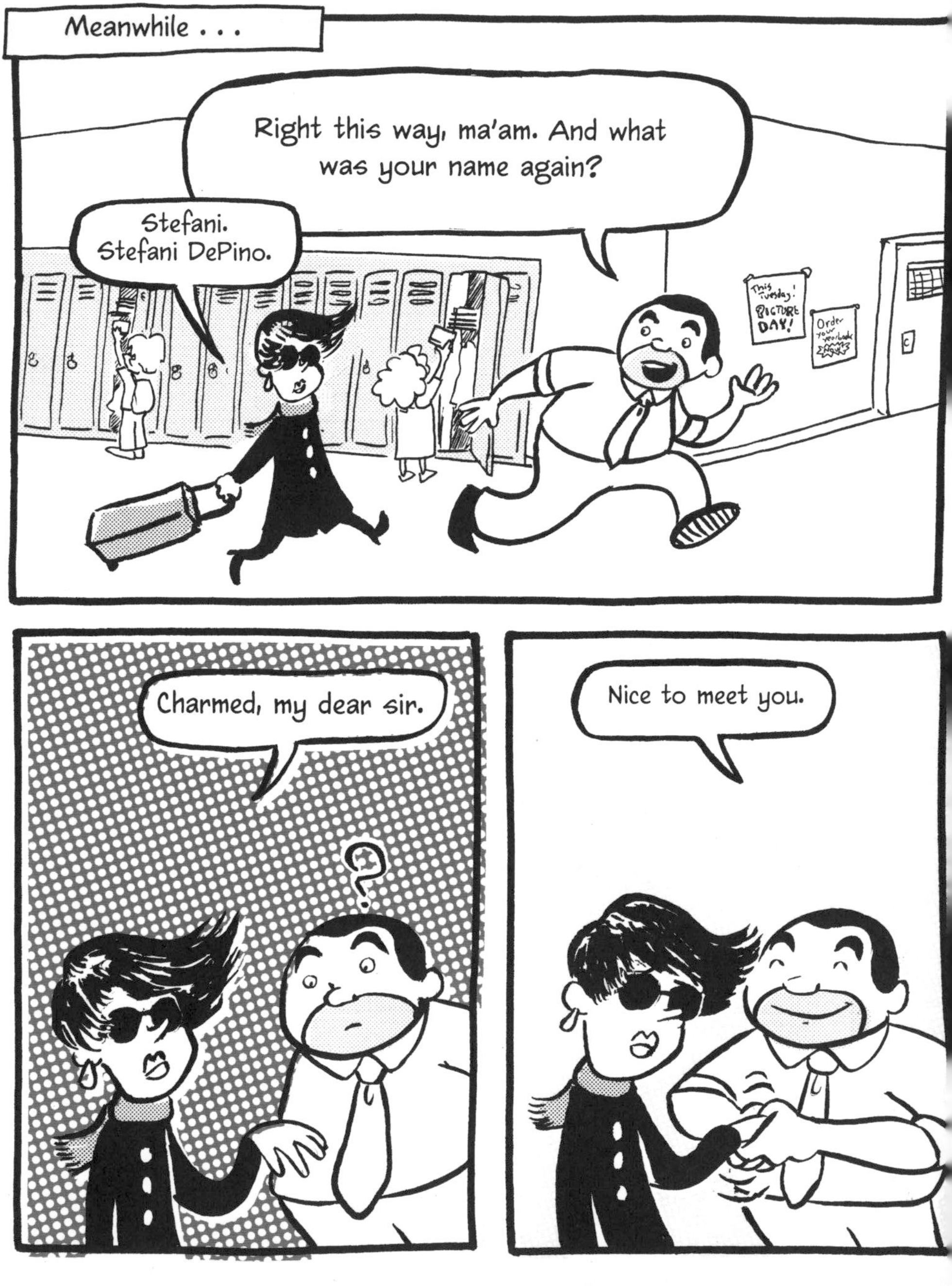
Meanwhile . . .
Right this way, ma'am. And what was your name again?
Stefani. Stefani DePino.
This Tuesday! PICTURE DAY!
Order your yearbook
Charmed, my dear sir.
Nice to meet you.

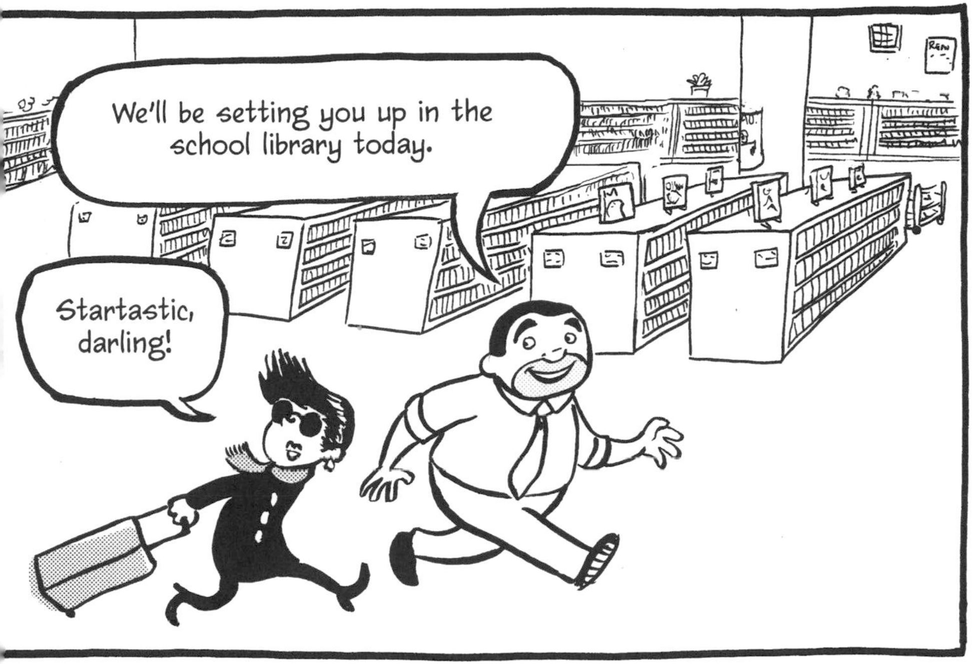
We'll be setting you up in the school library today.
Startastic, darling!

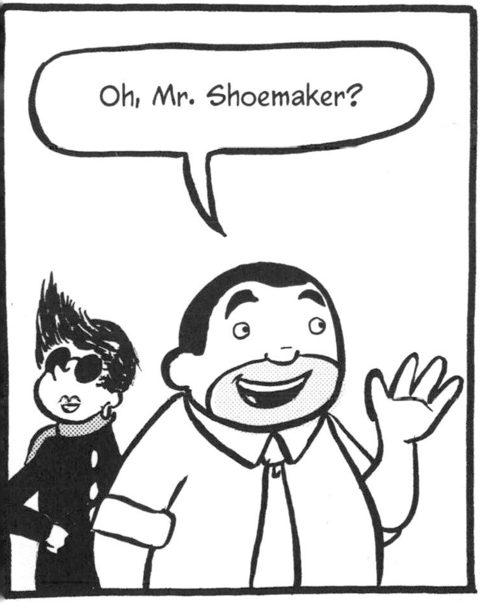
Oh, Mr. Shoemaker?

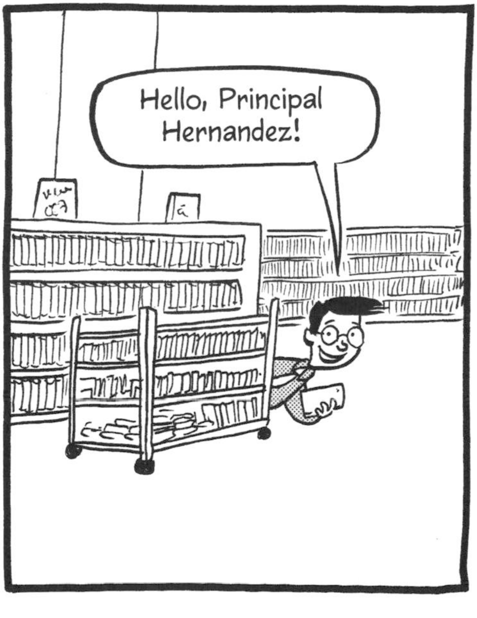
Hello, Principal Hernandez!

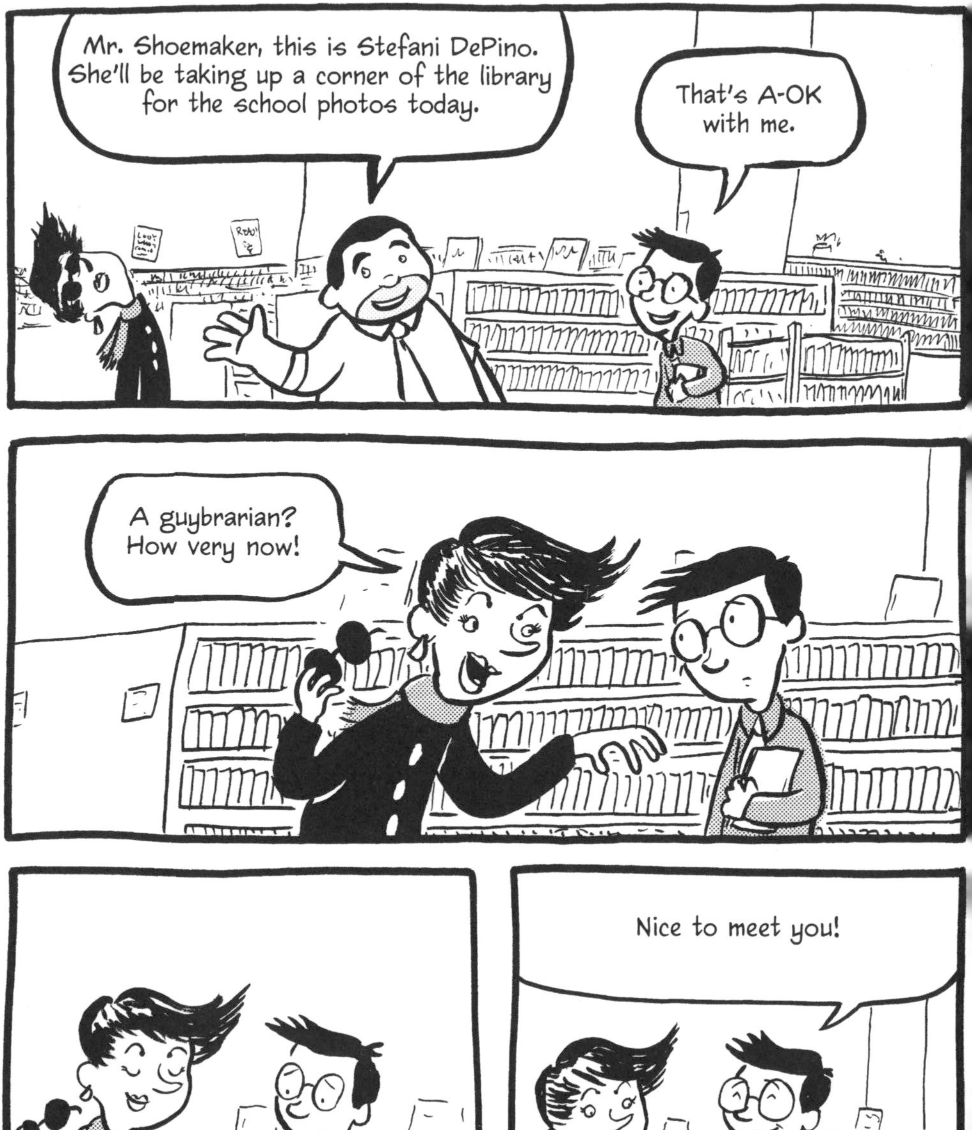
Mr. Shoemaker, this is Stefani DePino. She'll be taking up a corner of the library for the school photos today.
That's A-OK with me.
A guybrarian? How very now!
Nice to meet you!

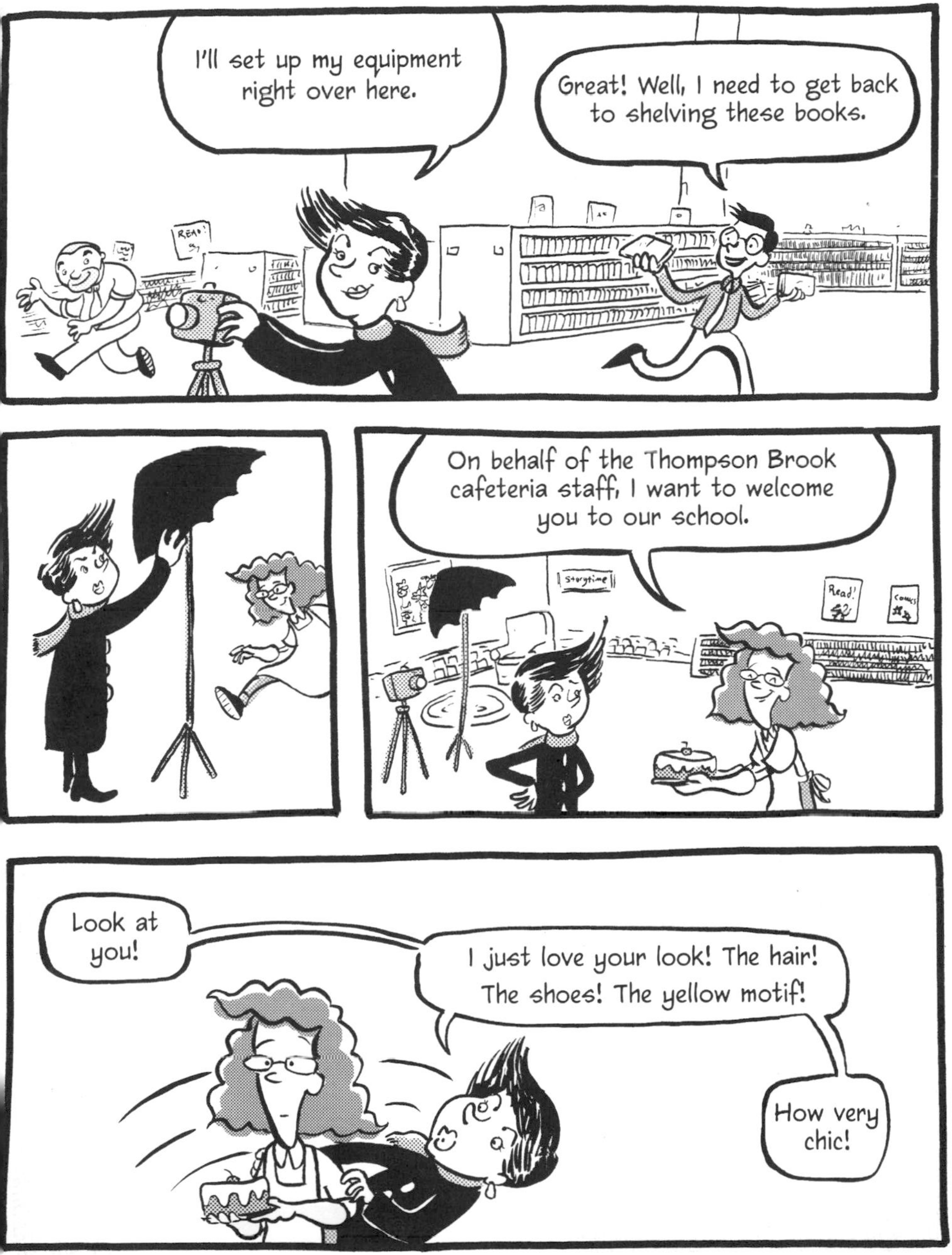
I'll set up my equipment right over here.
Great! Well, I need to get back to shelving these books.
On behalf of the Thompson Brook cafeteria staff, I want to welcome you to our school.
Look at you!
I just love your look! The hair! The shoes! The yellow motif!
How very chic!

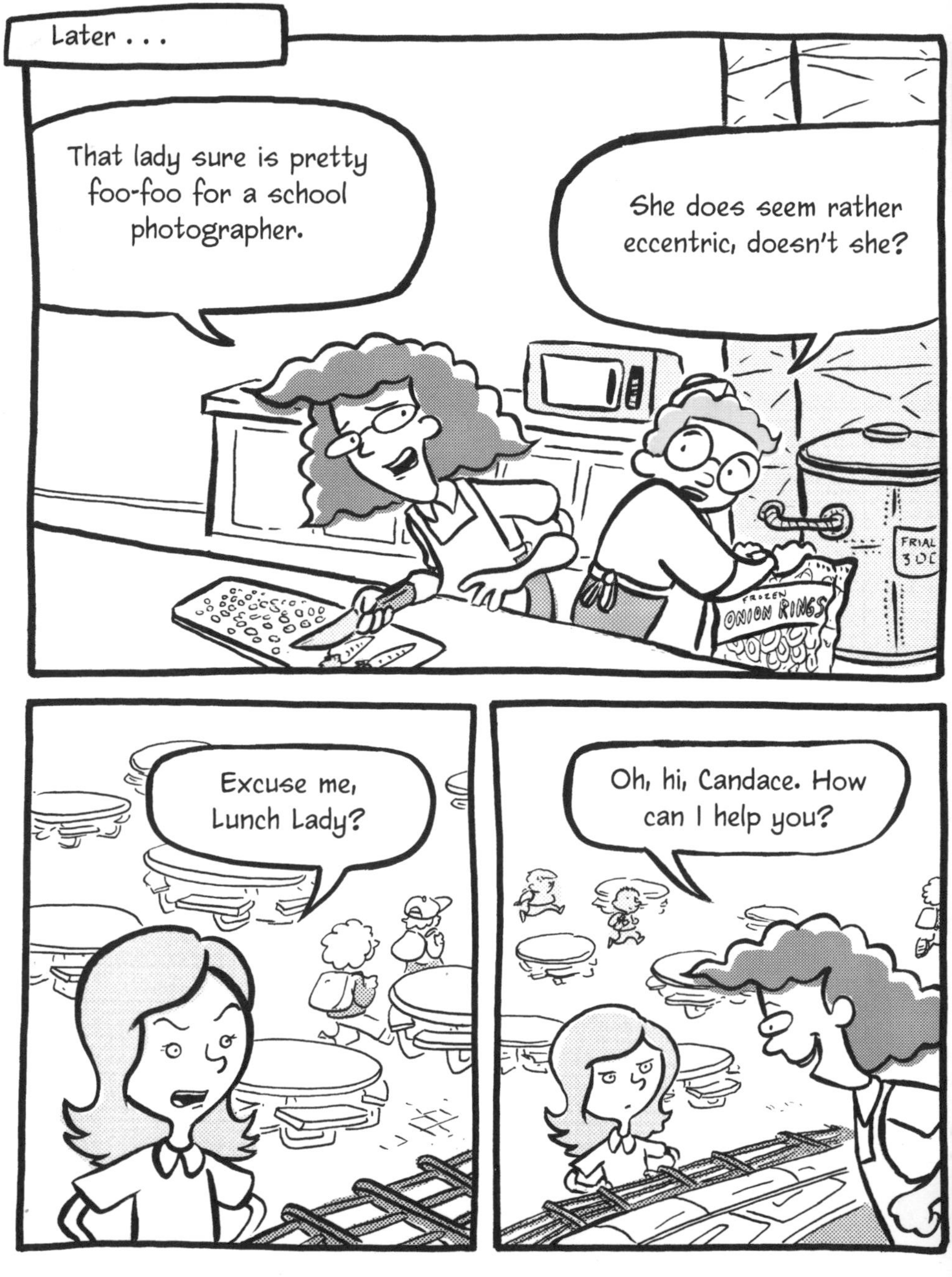

Later . . .
That lady sure is pretty foo-foo for a school photographer.
She does seem rather eccentric, doesn't she?
FROZEN ONION RINGS
Excuse me, Lunch Lady?
Oh, hi, Candace. How can I help you?

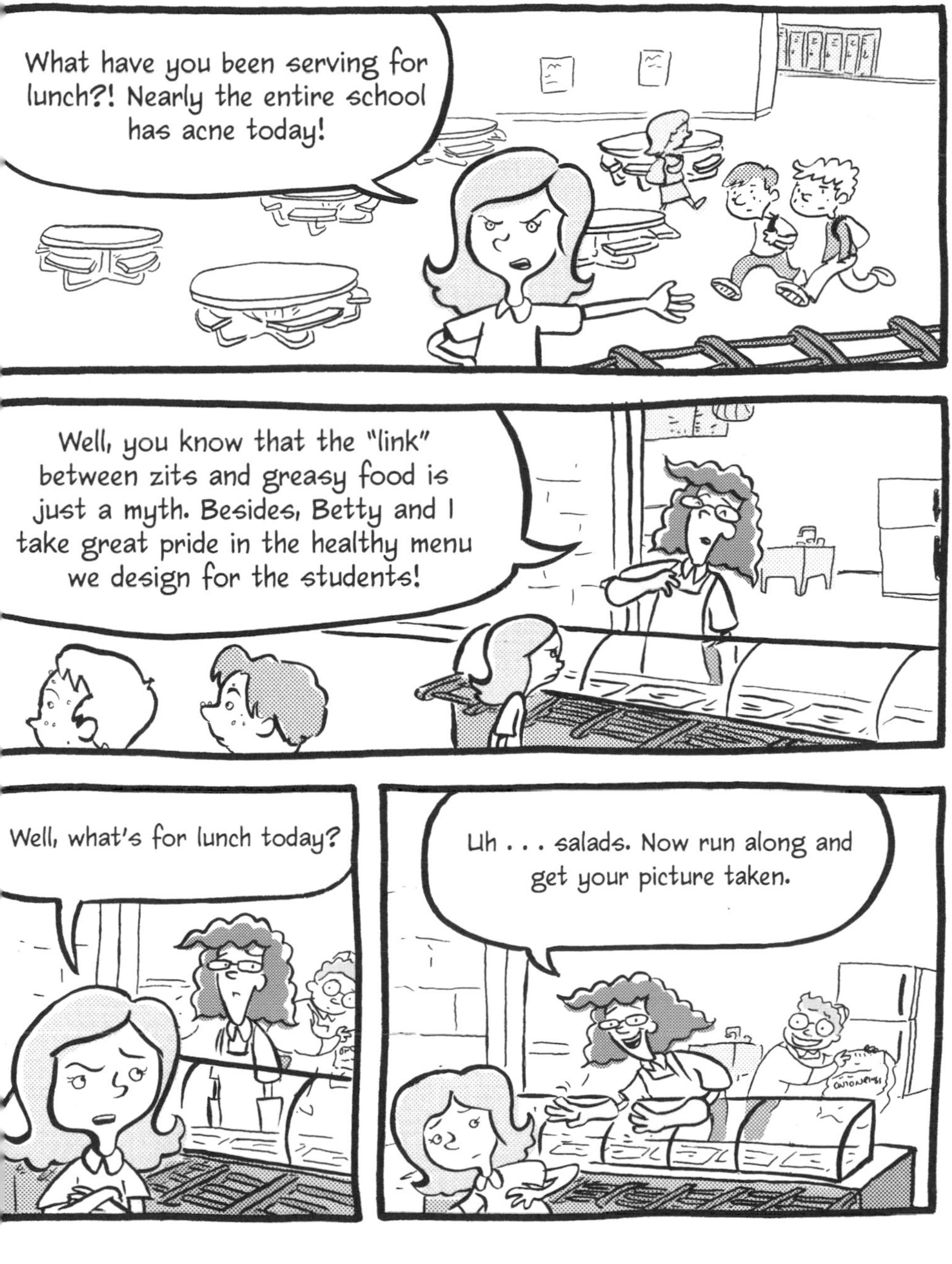
What have you been serving for lunch?! Nearly the entire school has acne today!
Well, you know that the "link" between zits and greasy food is just a myth. Besides, Betty and I take great pride in the healthy menu we design for the students!
Well, what's for lunch today?
Uh . . . salads. Now run along and get your picture taken.

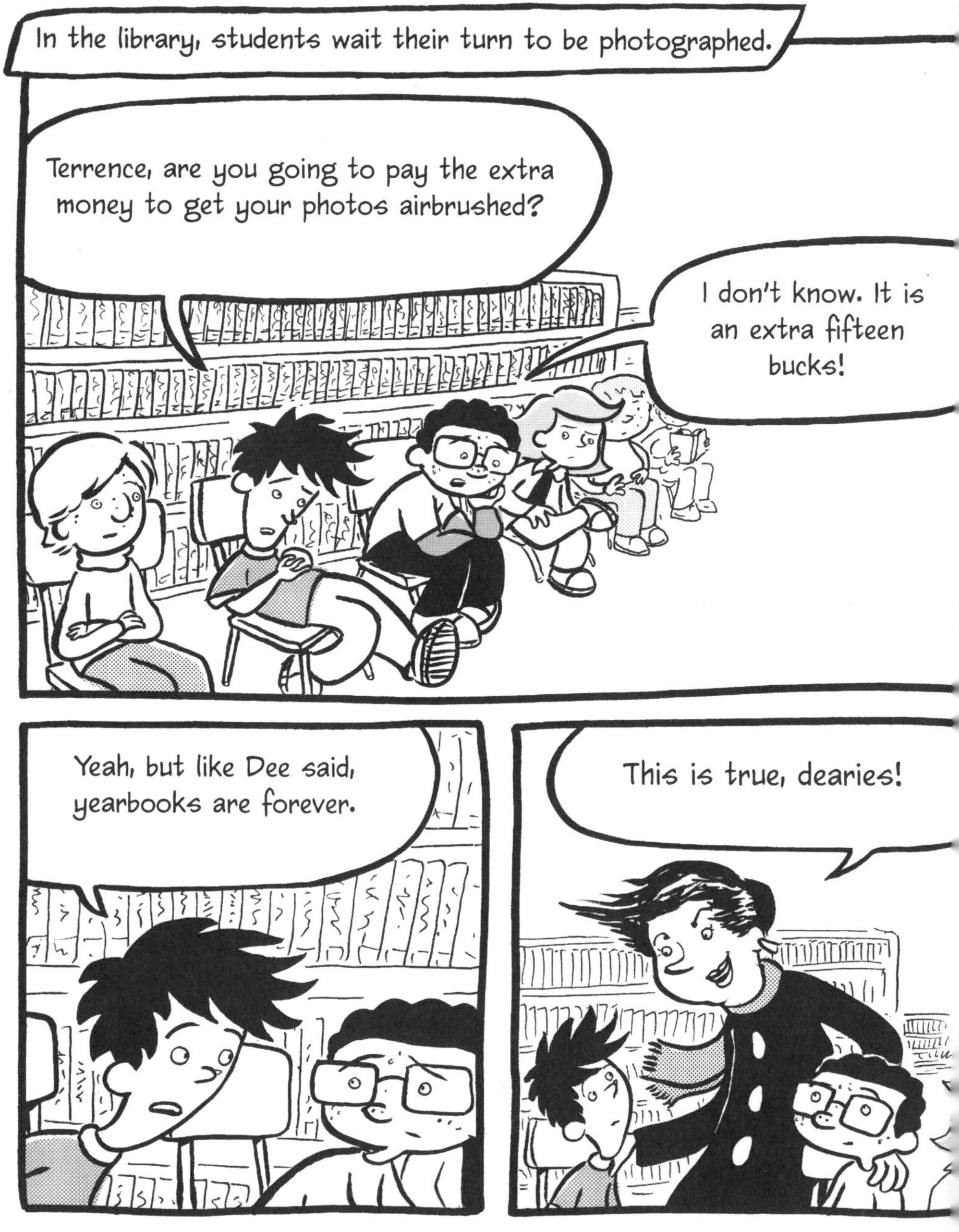
In the library, students wait their turn to be photographed.
Terrence, are you going to pay the extra money to get your photos airbrushed?
I don't know. It is an extra fifteen bucks!
Yeah, but like Dee said, yearbooks are forever.
This is true, dearies!

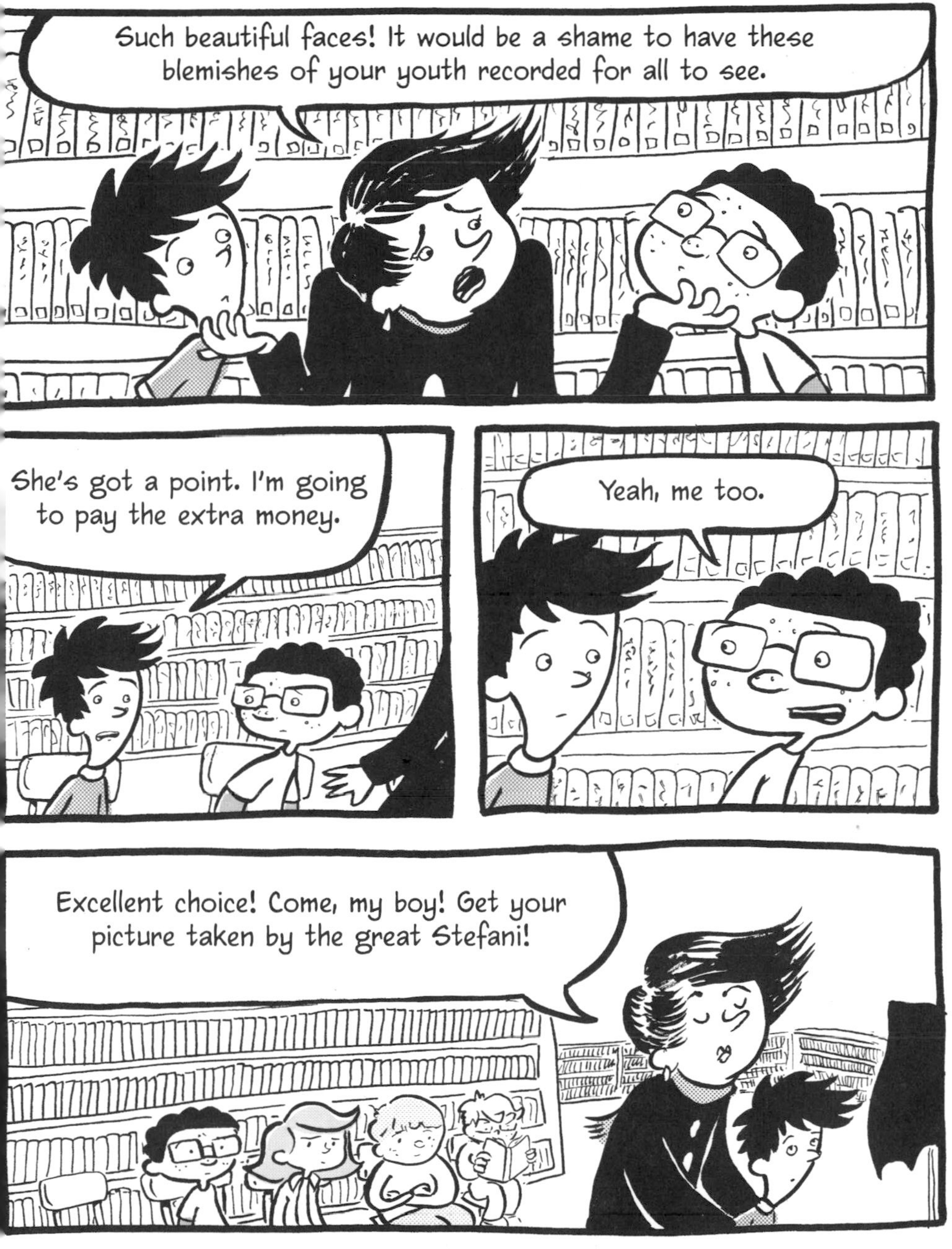
Such beautiful faces! It would be a shame to have these blemishes of your youth recorded for all to see.
She's got a point. I'm going to pay the extra money.
Yeah, me too.
Excellent choice! Come, my boy! Get your picture taken by the great Stefani!

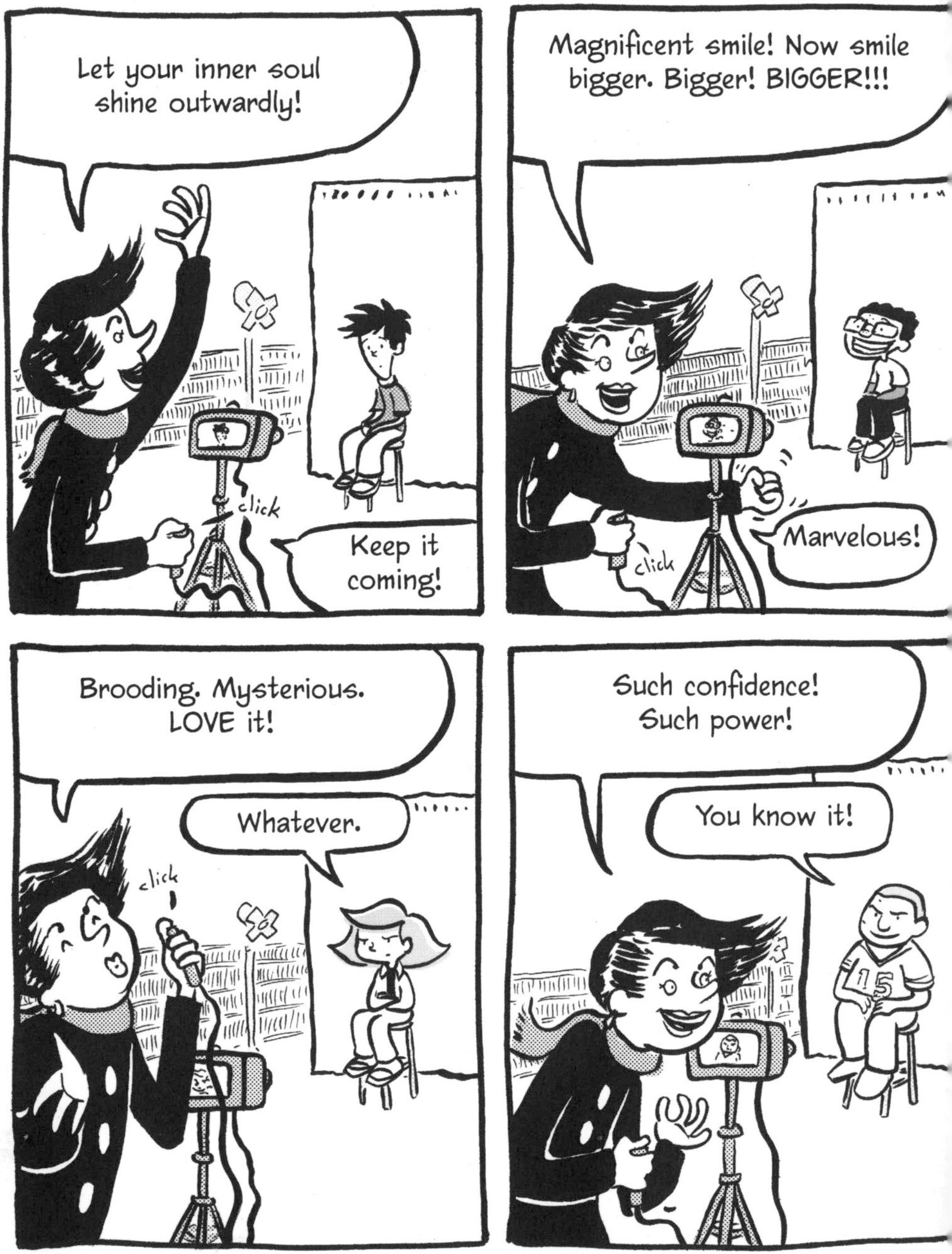
Let your inner soul shine outwardly!
click
Keep it coming!
Magnificent smile! Now smile bigger. Bigger! BIGGER!!!
click
Marvelous!
Brooding. Mysterious. LOVE it!
Whatever.
click
Such confidence! Such power!
You know it!

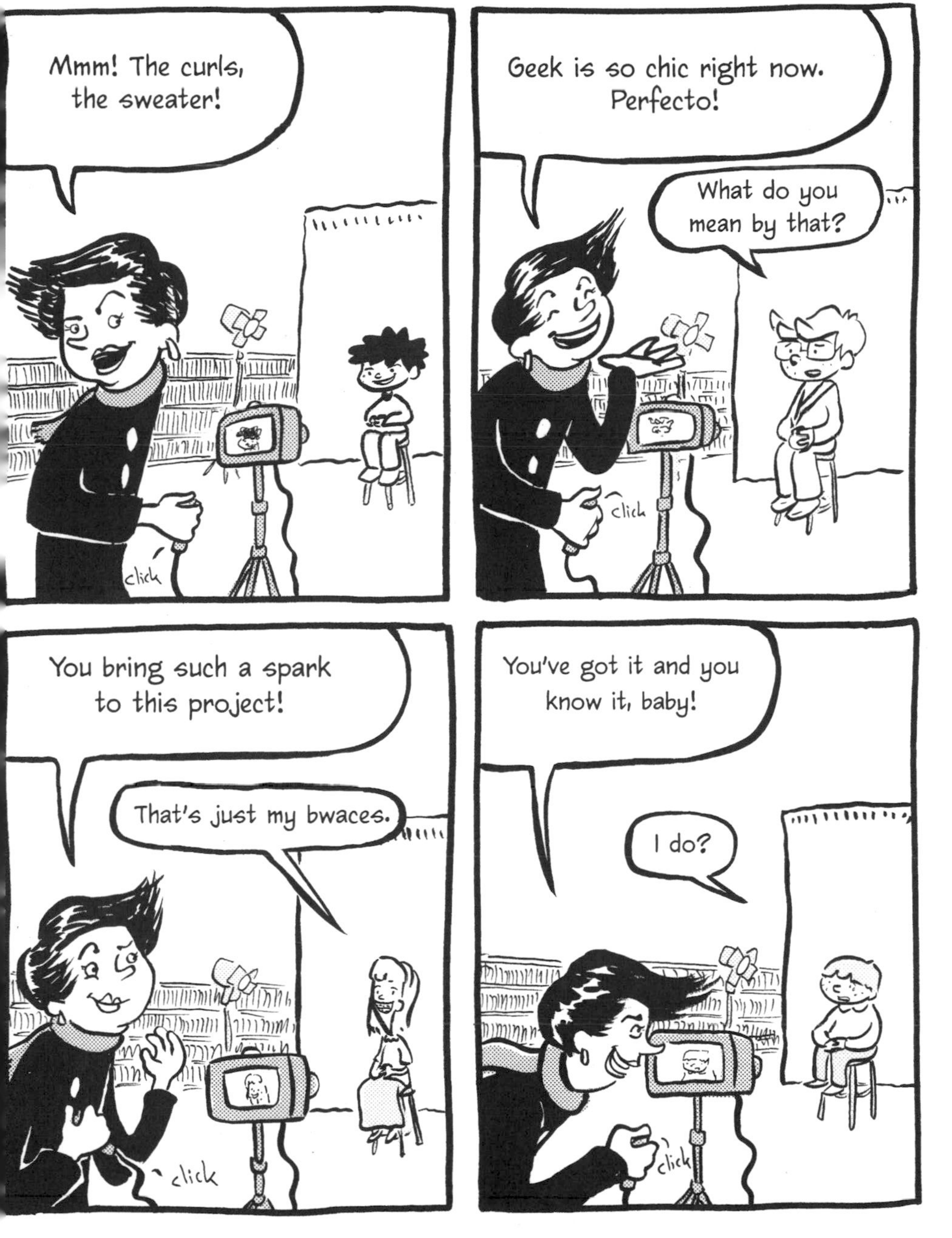
Mmm! The curls, the sweater!
click
Geek is so chic right now. Perfecto!
What do you mean by that?
click
You bring such a spark to this project!
That's just my bwaces.
click
You've got it and you know it, baby!
I do?
click

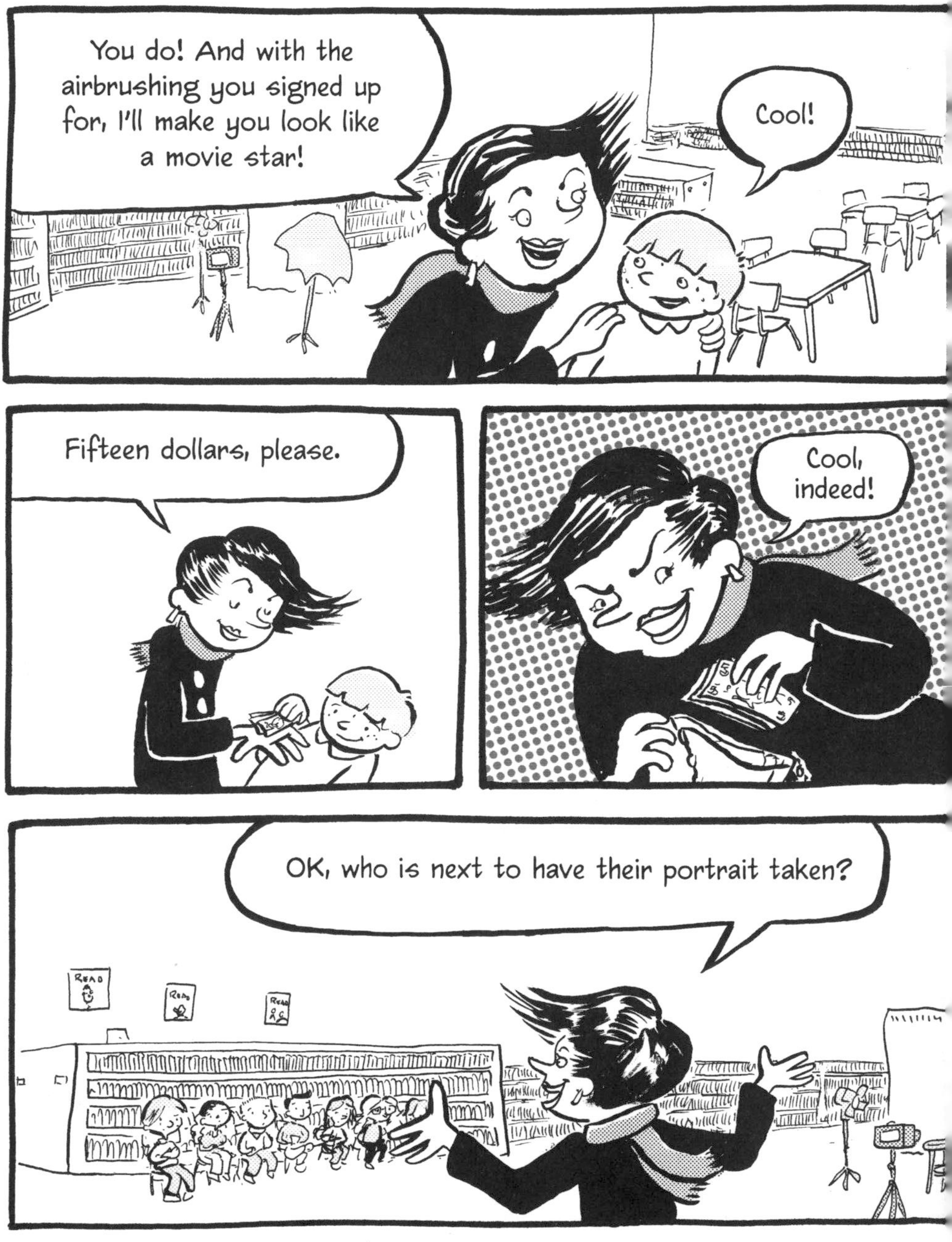
You do! And with the airbrushing you signed up for, I'll make you look like a movie star!
Cool!
Fifteen dollars, please.
Cool, indeed!
OK, who is next to have their portrait taken?

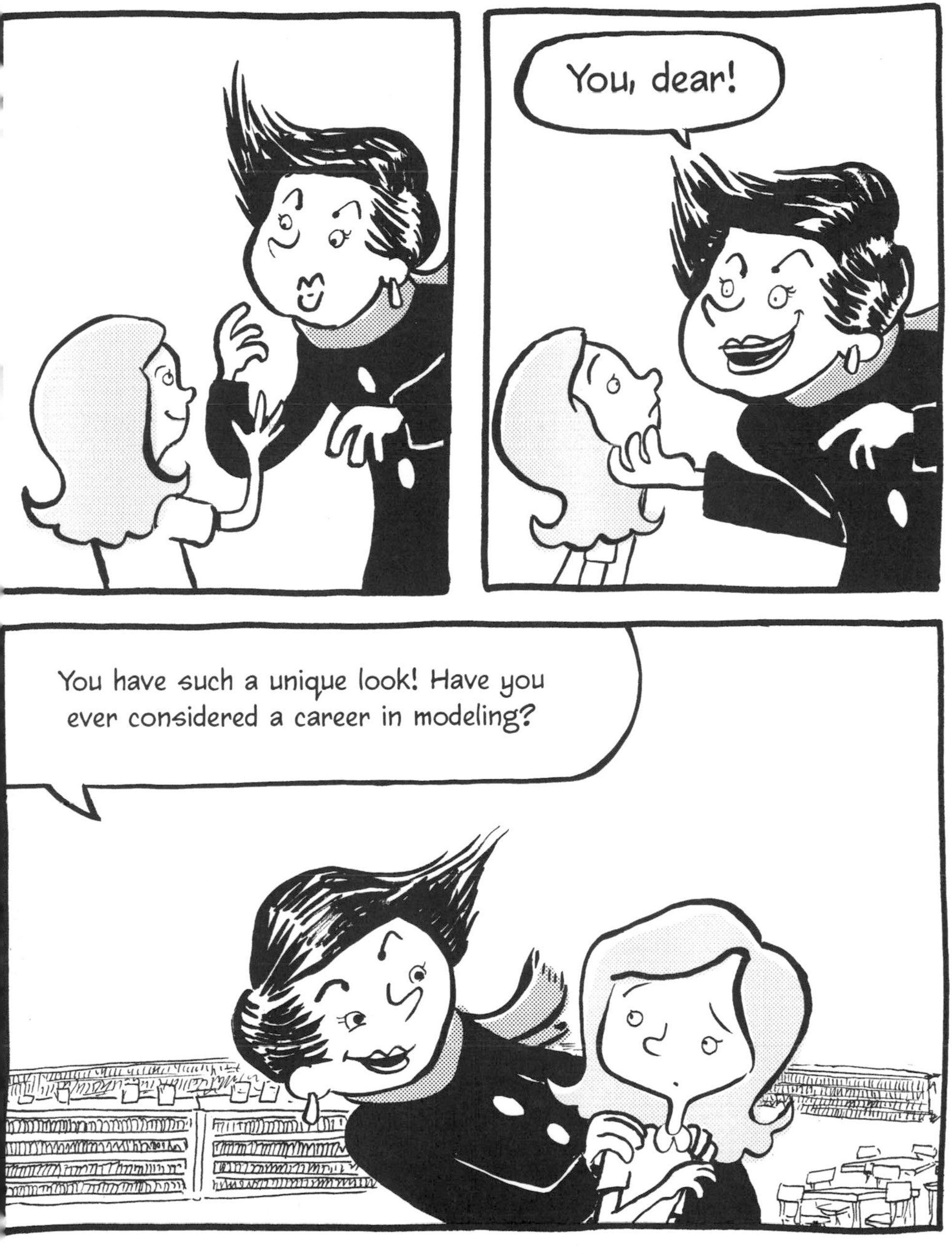
You, dear!
You have such a unique look! Have you ever considered a career in modeling?

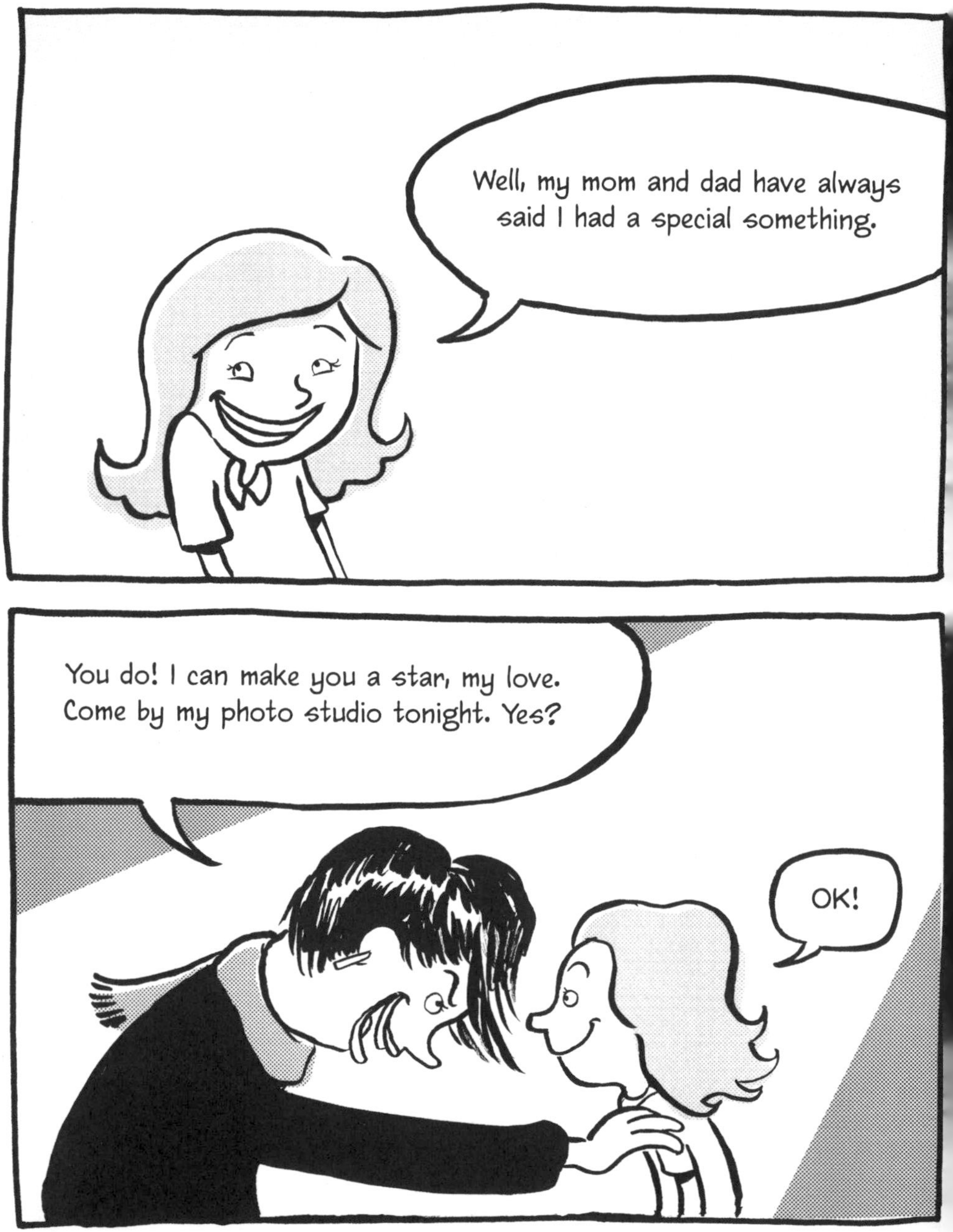
Well, my mom and dad have always said I had a special something.
You do! I can make you a star, my love. Come by my photo studio tonight. Yes?
OK!

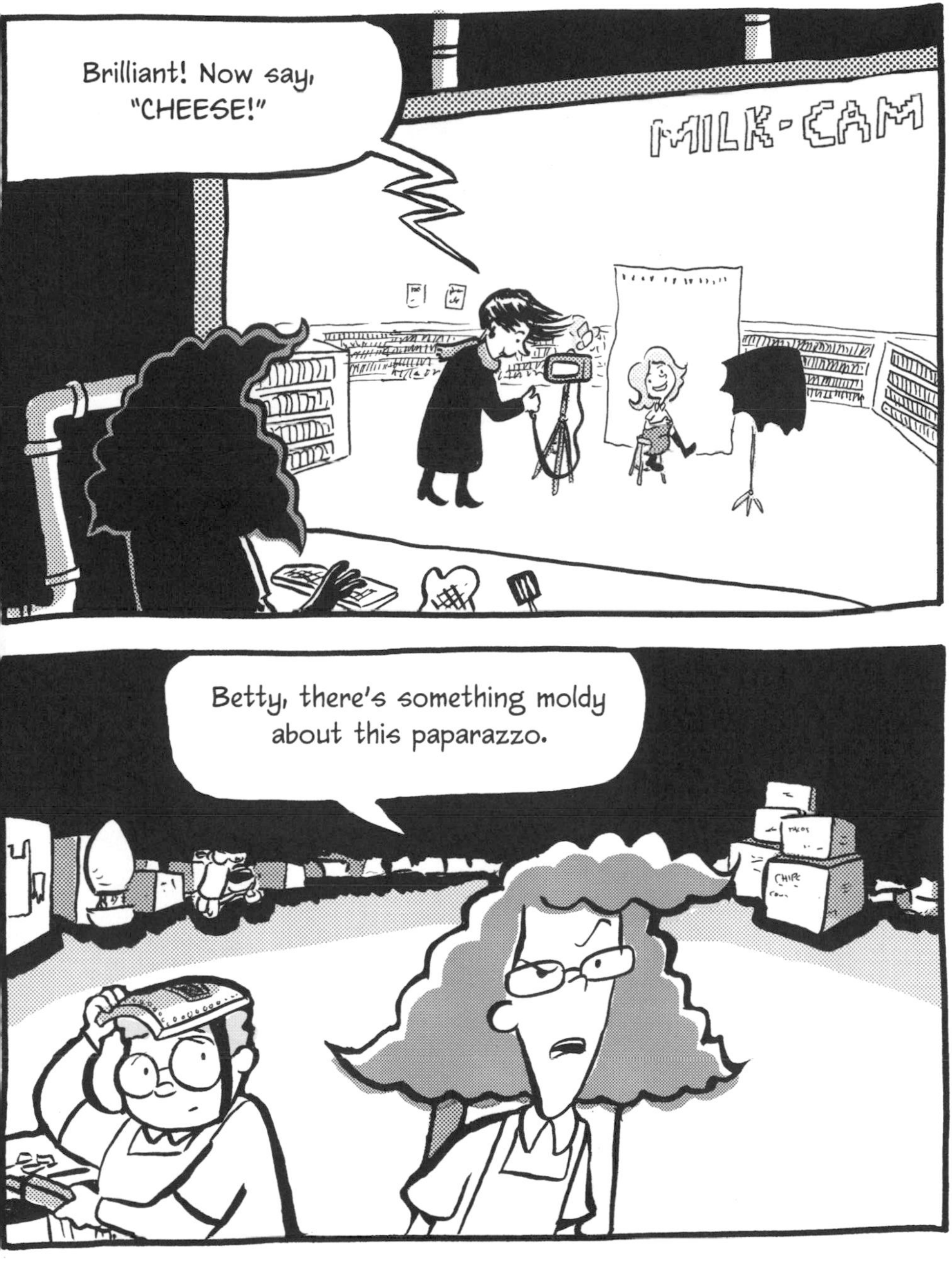
Brilliant! Now say, "CHEESE!"
MILK-CAM
Betty, there's something moldy about this paparazzo.

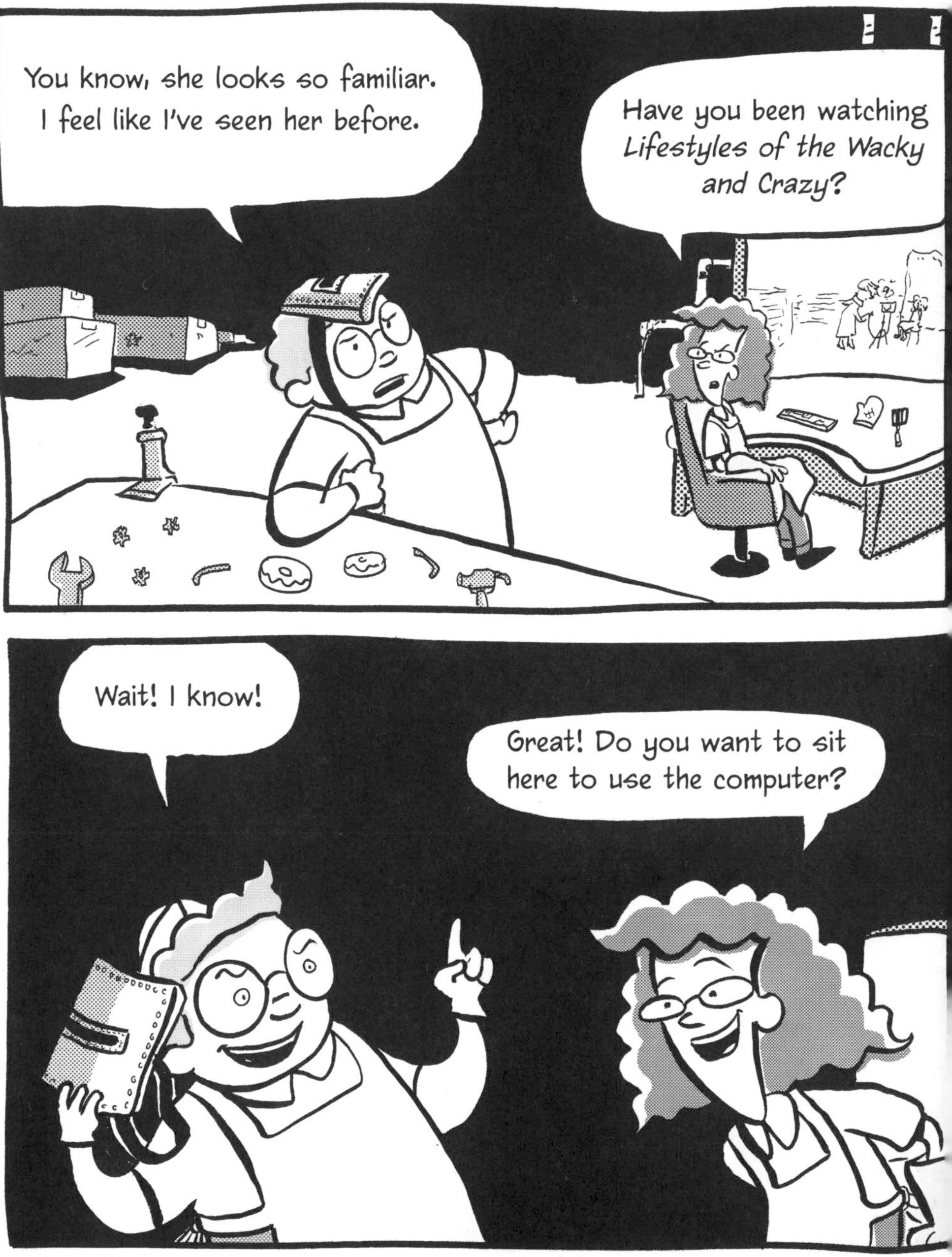
You know, she looks so familiar. I feel like I've seen her before.
Have you been watching *Lifestyles of the Wacky and Crazy?*
Wait! I know!
Great! Do you want to sit here to use the computer?

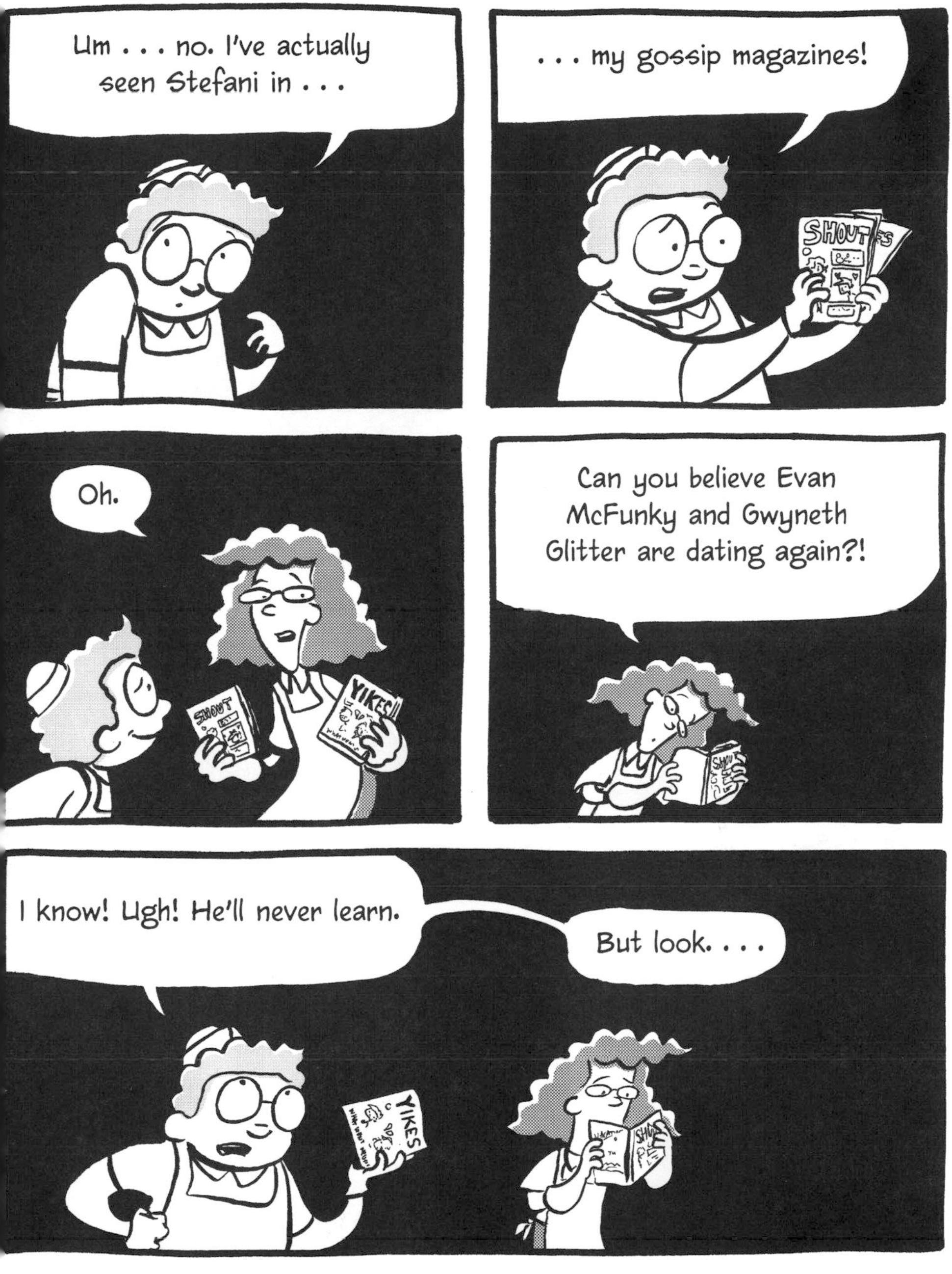
Um . . . no. I've actually seen Stefani in . . .
. . . my gossip magazines!
SHOUT
Oh.
SHOUT
YIKES!!
Can you believe Evan McFunky and Gwyneth Glitter are dating again?!
I know! Ugh! He'll never learn.
But look. . . .
YIKES

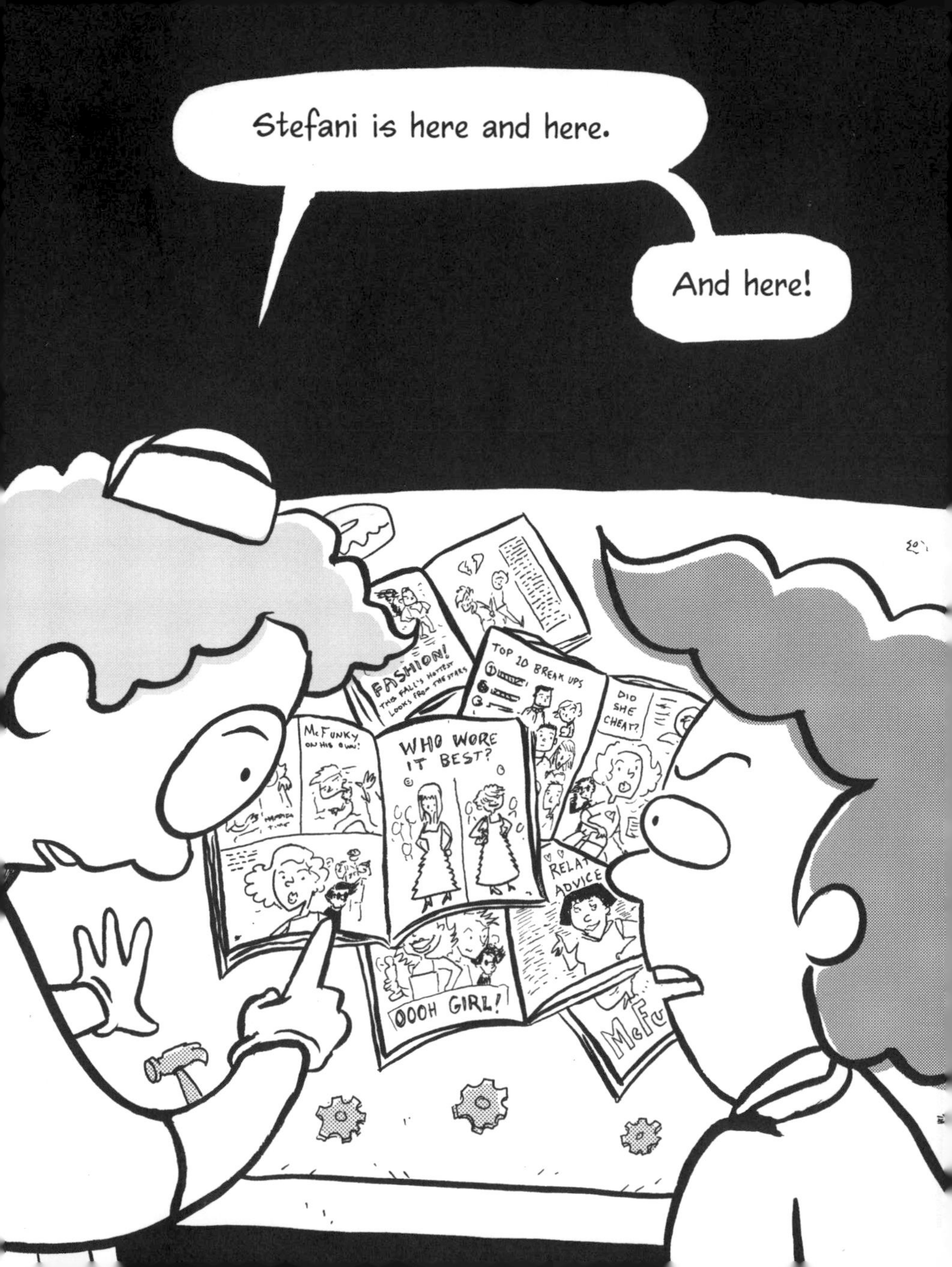

Stefani is here and here.
And here!
FASHION!
THIS FALL'S HOTTEST LOOKS FROM THE STARS
TOP 10 BREAK UPS
McFUNKY
ON HIS OWN!
WHO WORE IT BEST?
DID SHE CHEAT?
RELAT
ADVICE
OOOH GIRL!
McFu

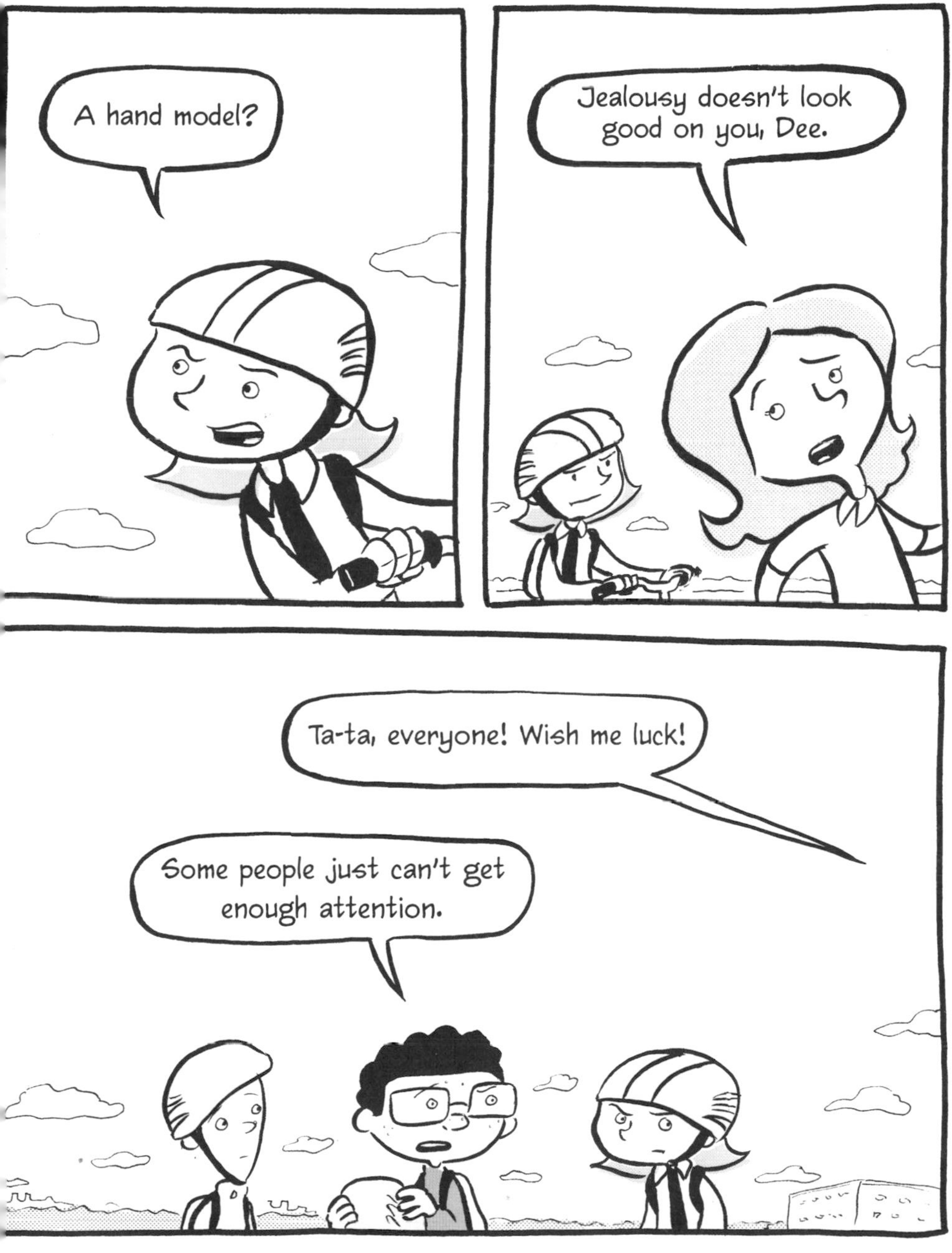
A hand model?
Jealousy doesn't look good on you, Dee.
Ta-ta, everyone! Wish me luck!
Some people just can't get enough attention.

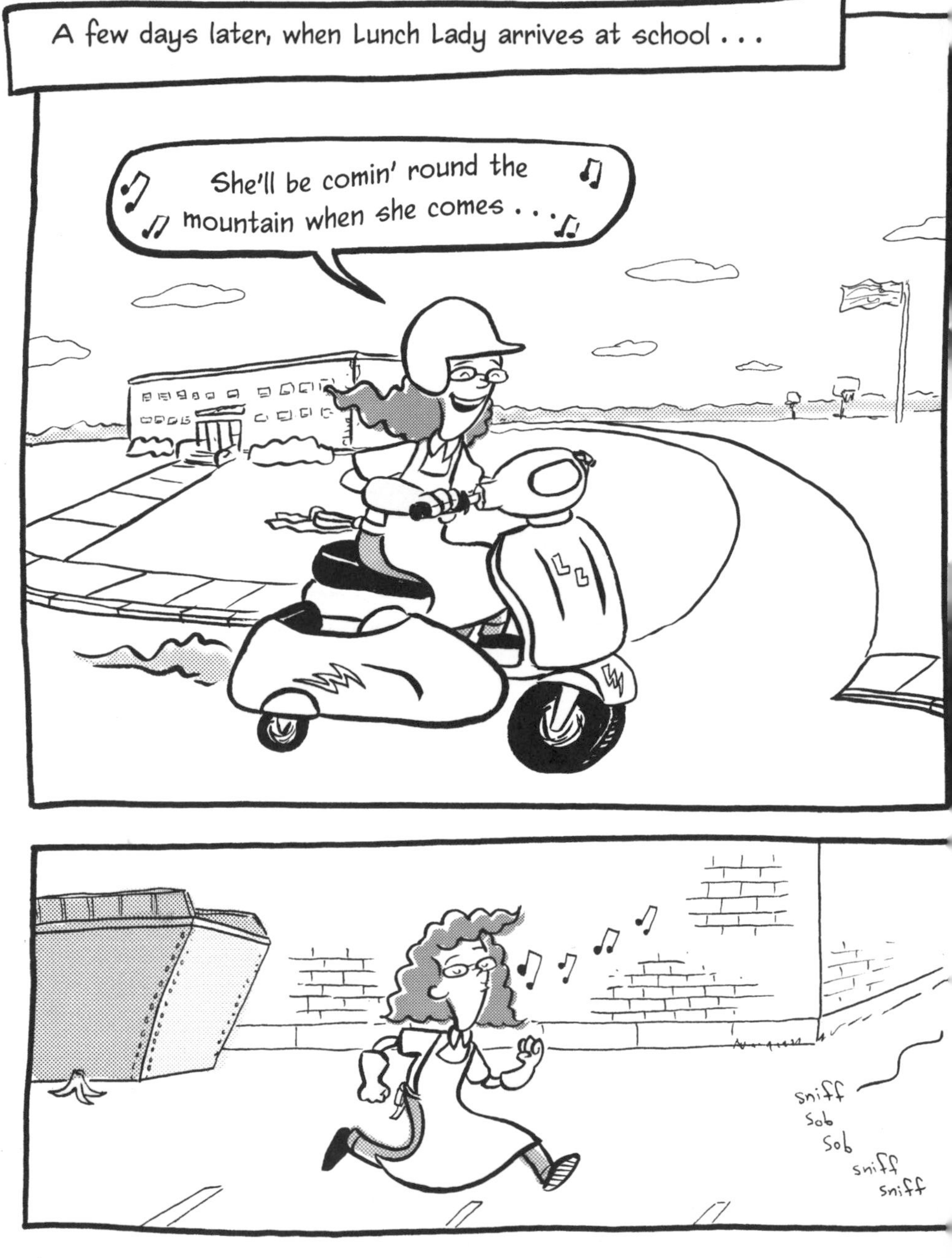
A few days later, when Lunch Lady arrives at school . . .
She'll be comin' round the mountain when she comes . . .
sniff
sob
sob
sniff
sniff

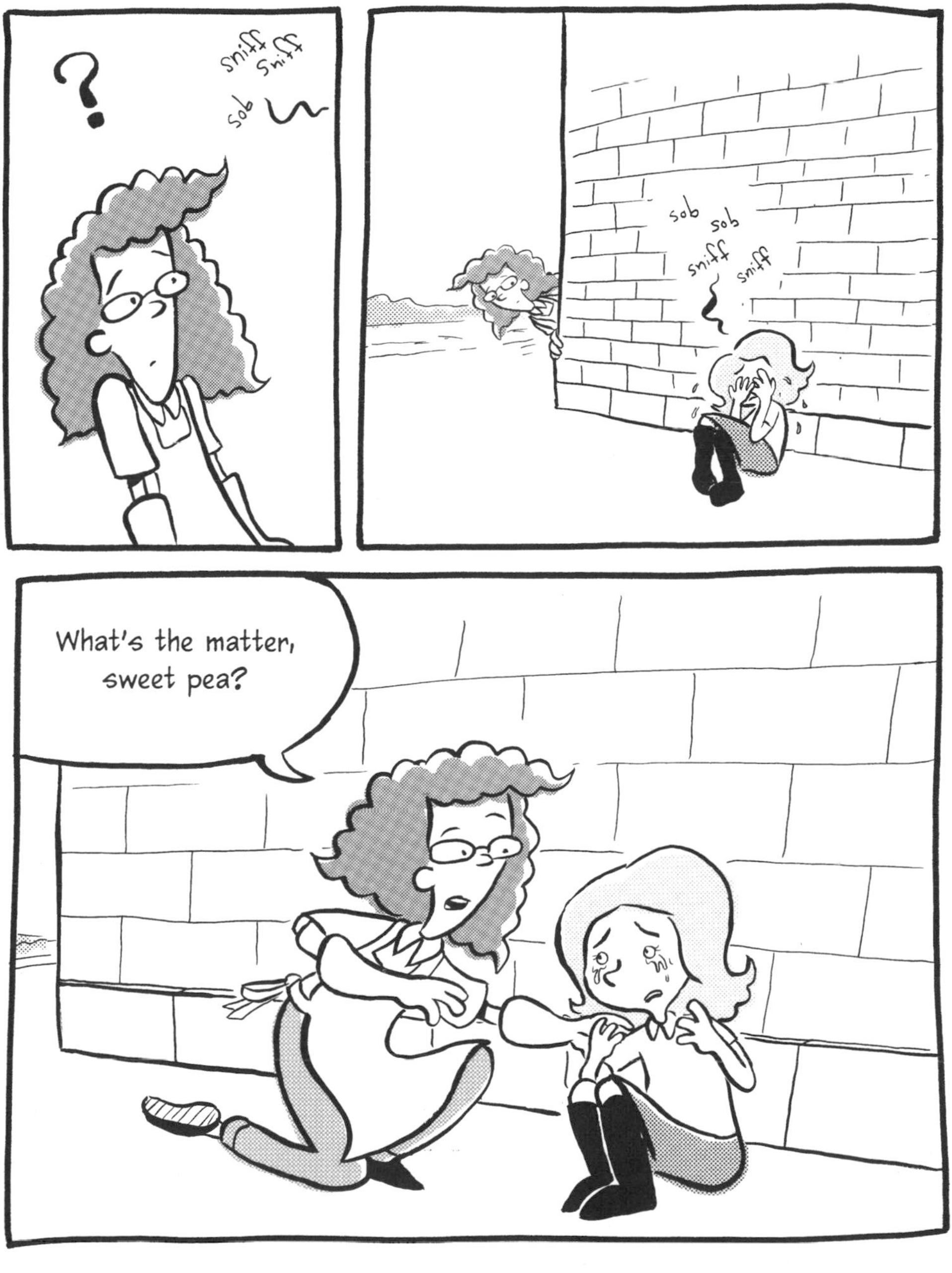
?
sniff sniff
sob
sob sob
sniff sniff
What's the matter, sweet pea?

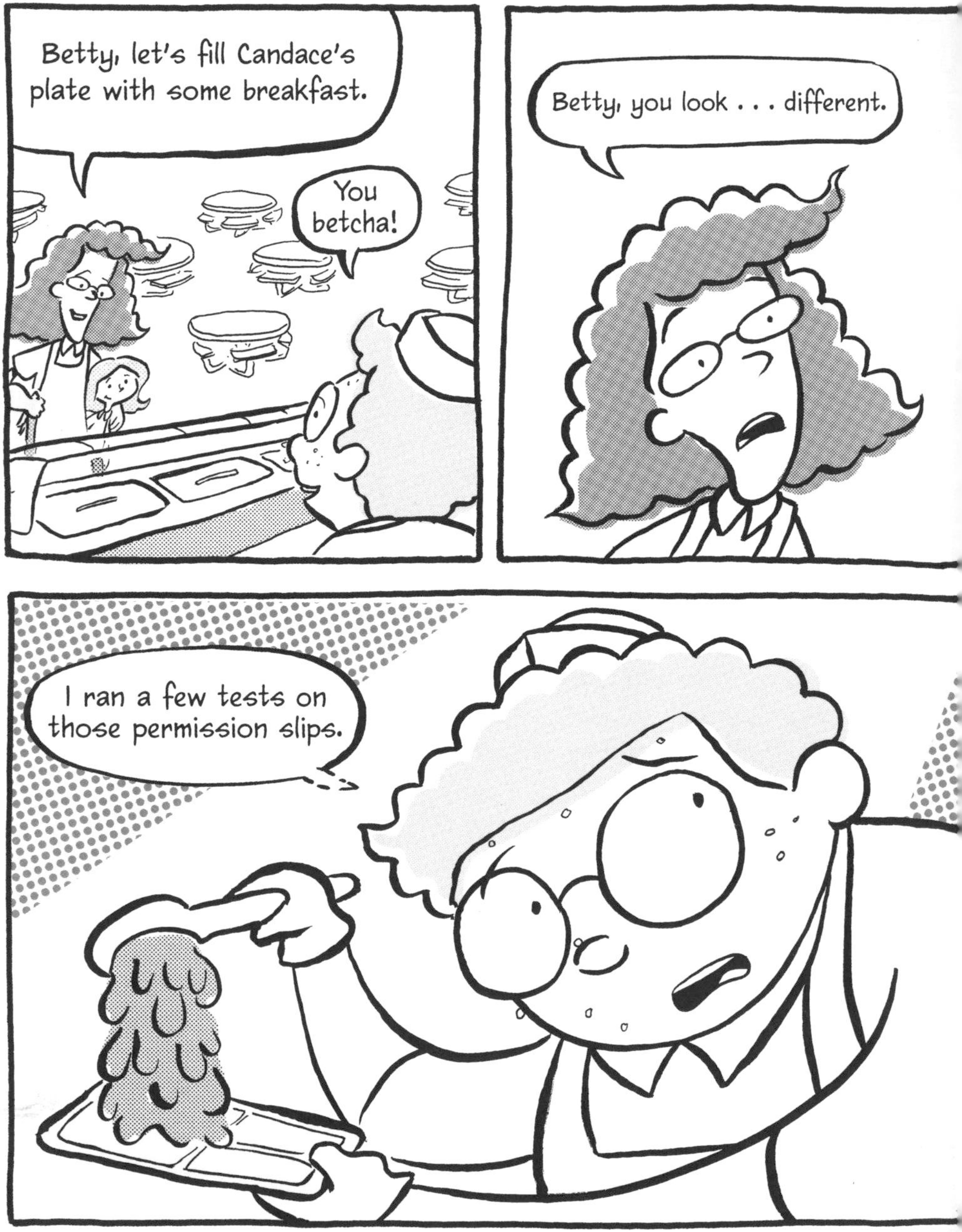
Betty, let's fill Candace's plate with some breakfast.
You betcha!
Betty, you look . . . different.
I ran a few tests on those permission slips.

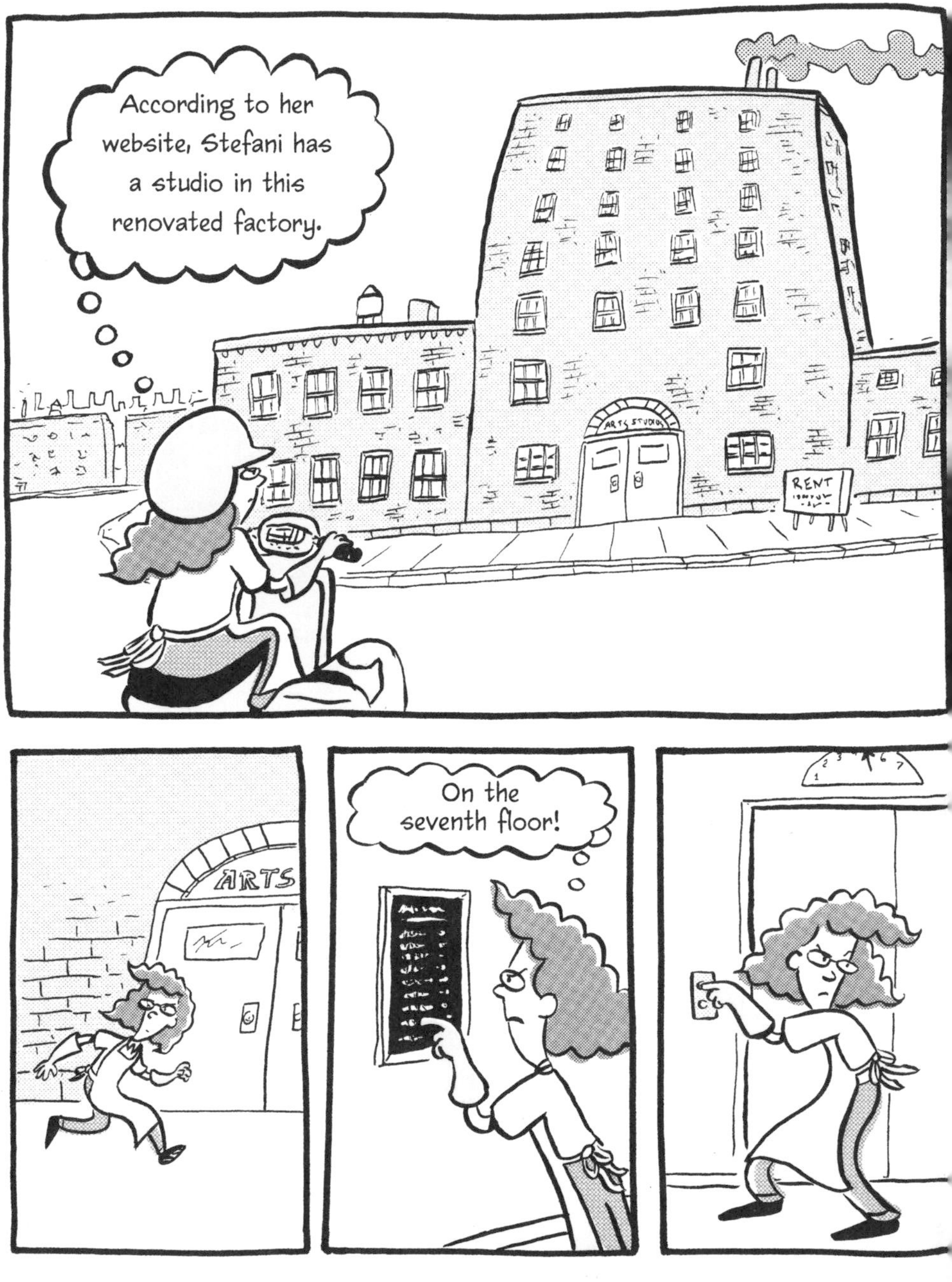
According to her website, Stefani has a studio in this renovated factory.
ARTS STUDIOS
RENT
ARTS
On the seventh floor!

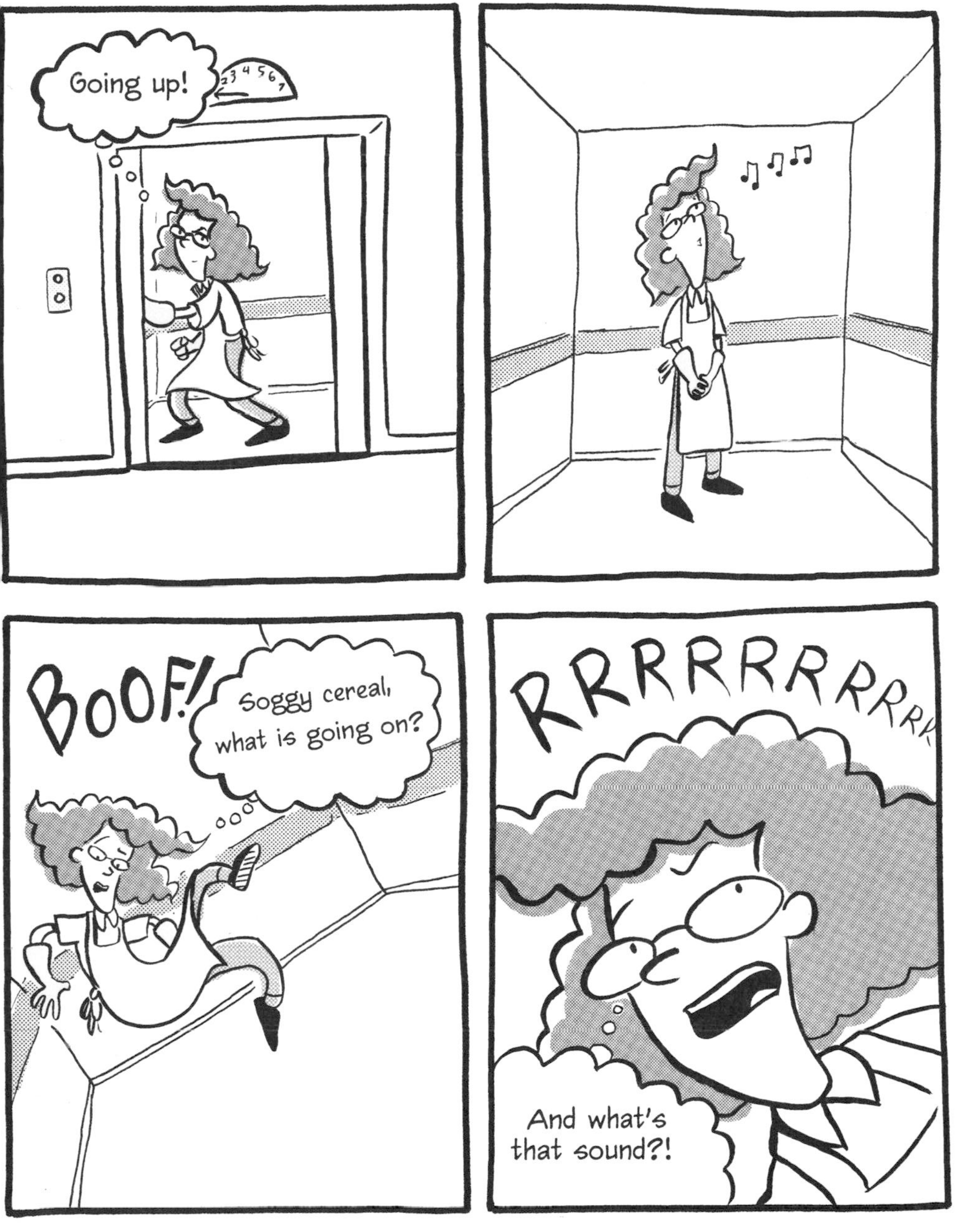
Going up!
1 2 3 4 5 6 7
BOOF!
Soggy cereal, what is going on?
RRRRRRRRRRRK
And what's that sound?!

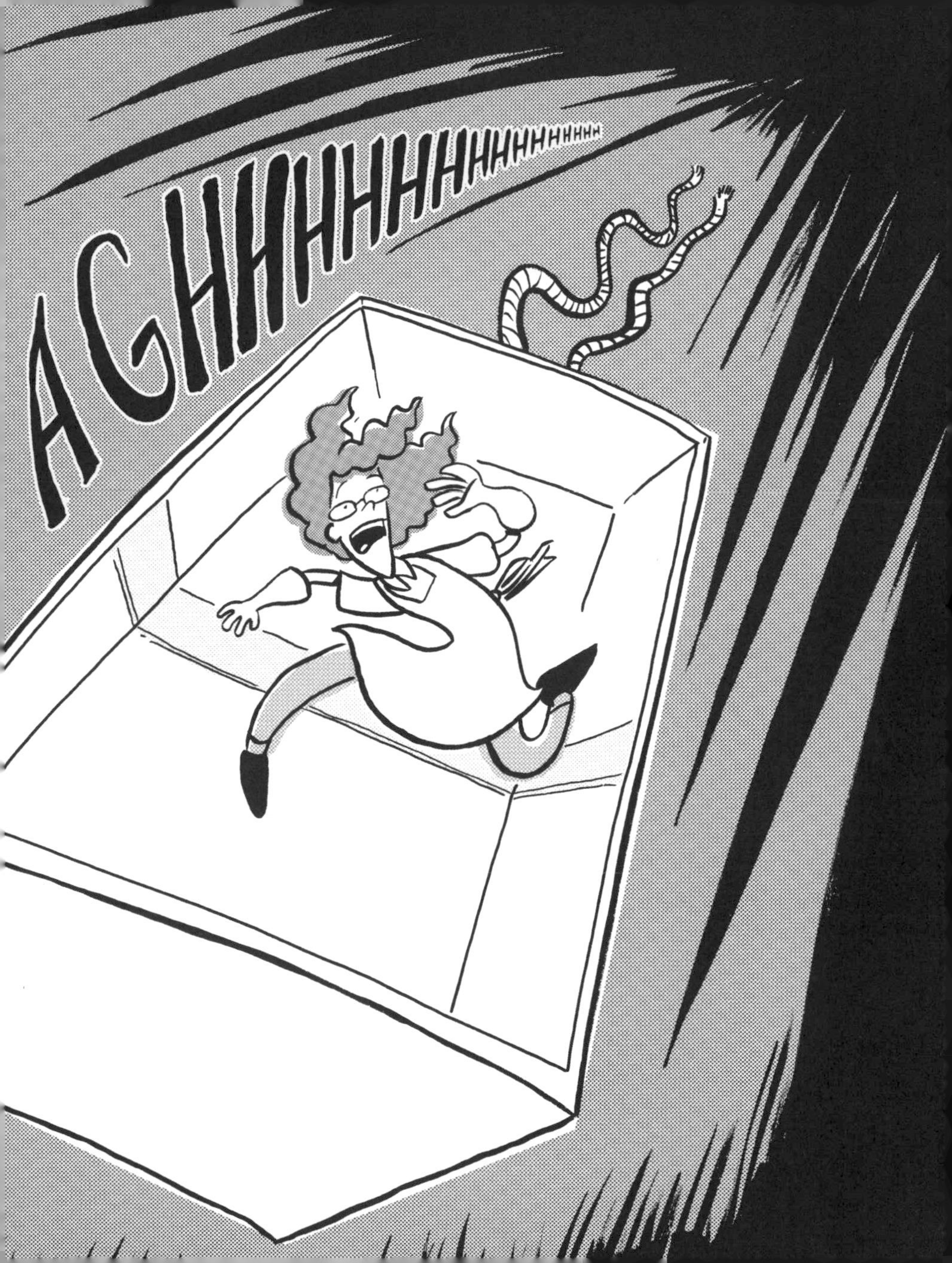
AGHHHHHHHHHHHHHHHH

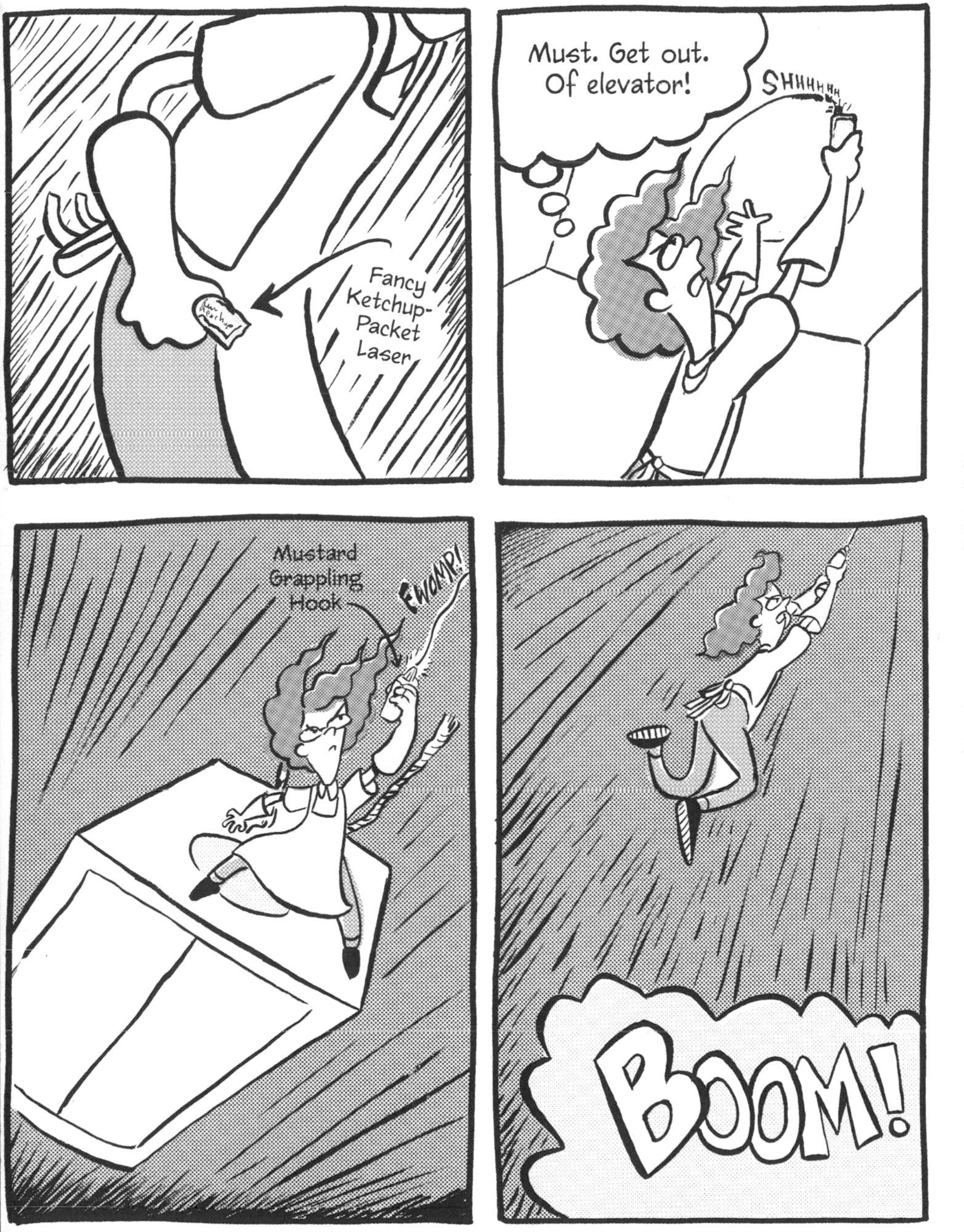

Fancy Ketchup-Packet Laser
Must. Get out. Of elevator!
SHHHHHHH
Mustard Grappling Hook
FWOMP!
BOOM!

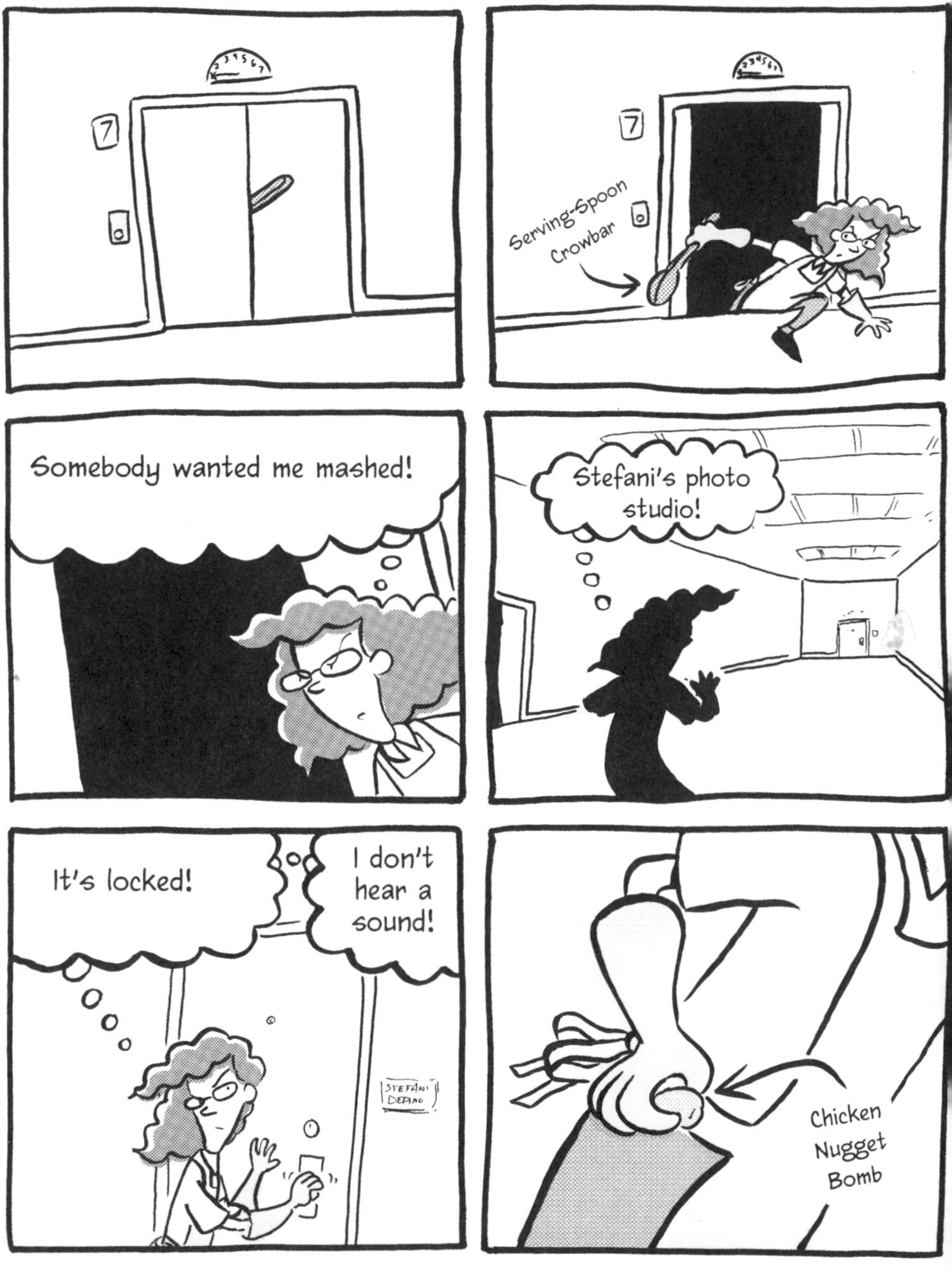
7
7
Serving-Spoon Crowbar
Somebody wanted me mashed!
Stefani's photo studio!
It's locked!
I don't hear a sound!
STEFANI DEPINO
Chicken Nugget Bomb

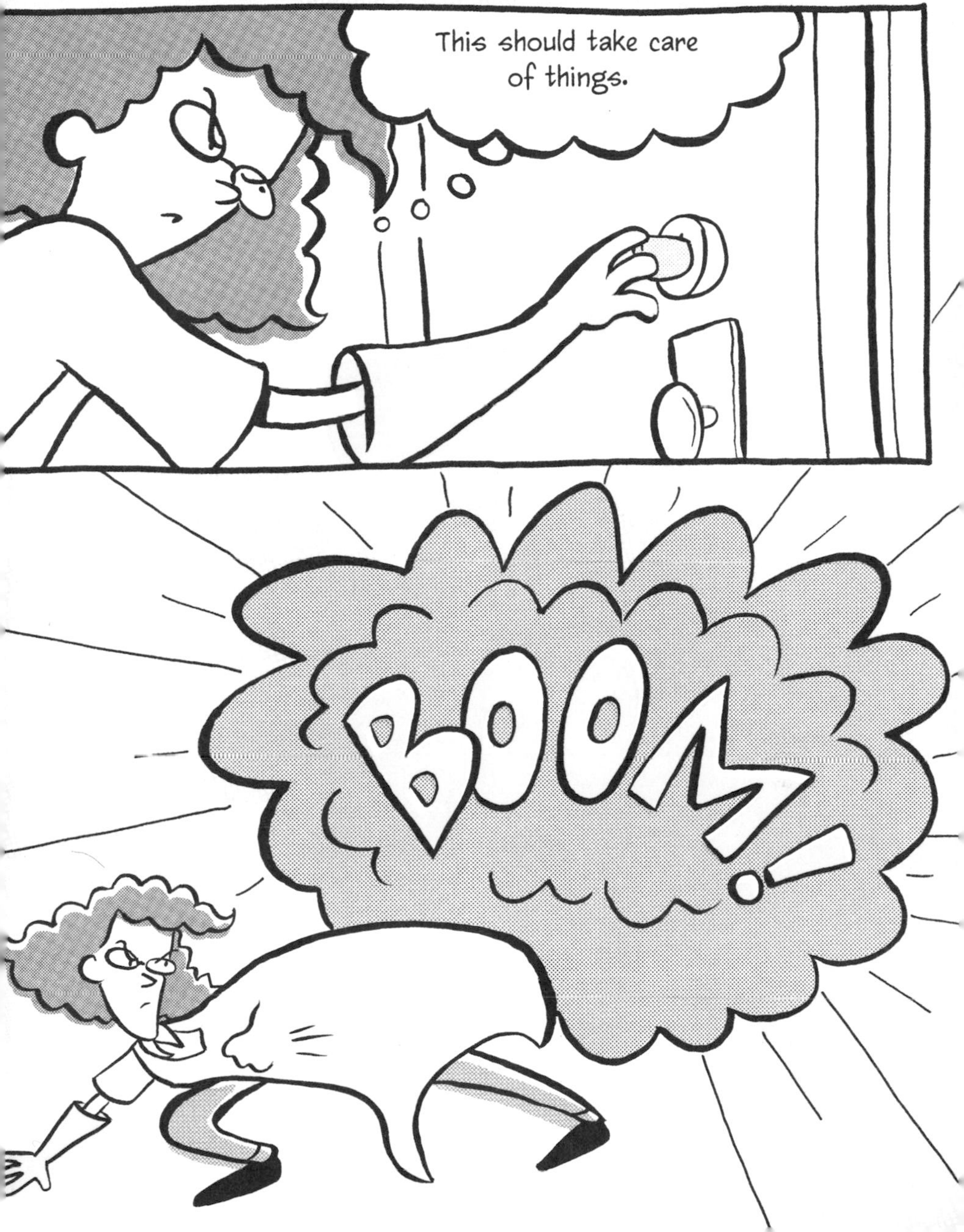
This should take care of things.
BOOM!

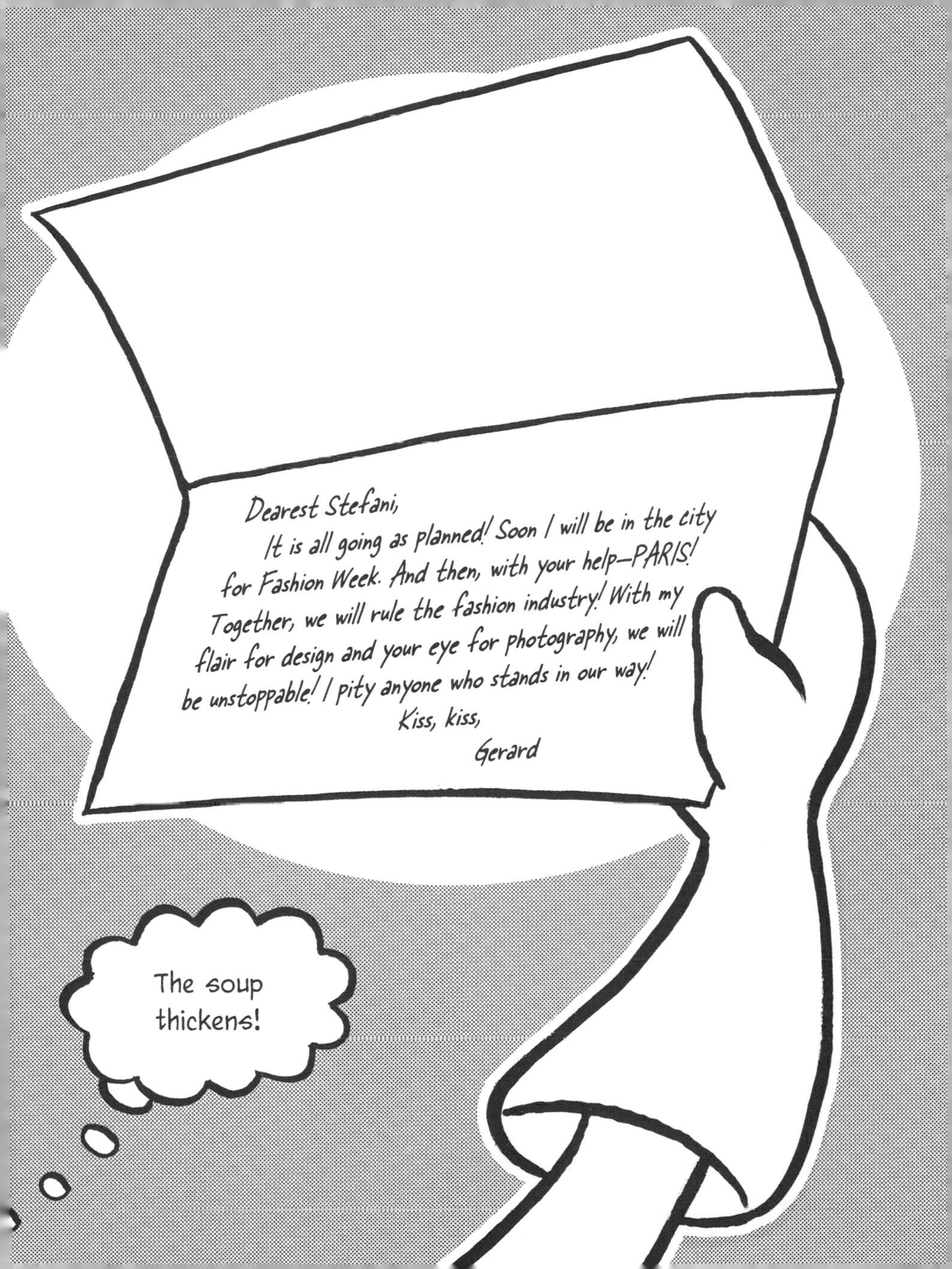
Dearest Stefani,
It is all going as planned! Soon I will be in the city for Fashion Week. And then, with your help—PARIS! Together, we will rule the fashion industry! With my flair for design and your eye for photography, we will be unstoppable! I pity anyone who stands in our way!
Kiss, kiss,
Gerard
The soup thickens!

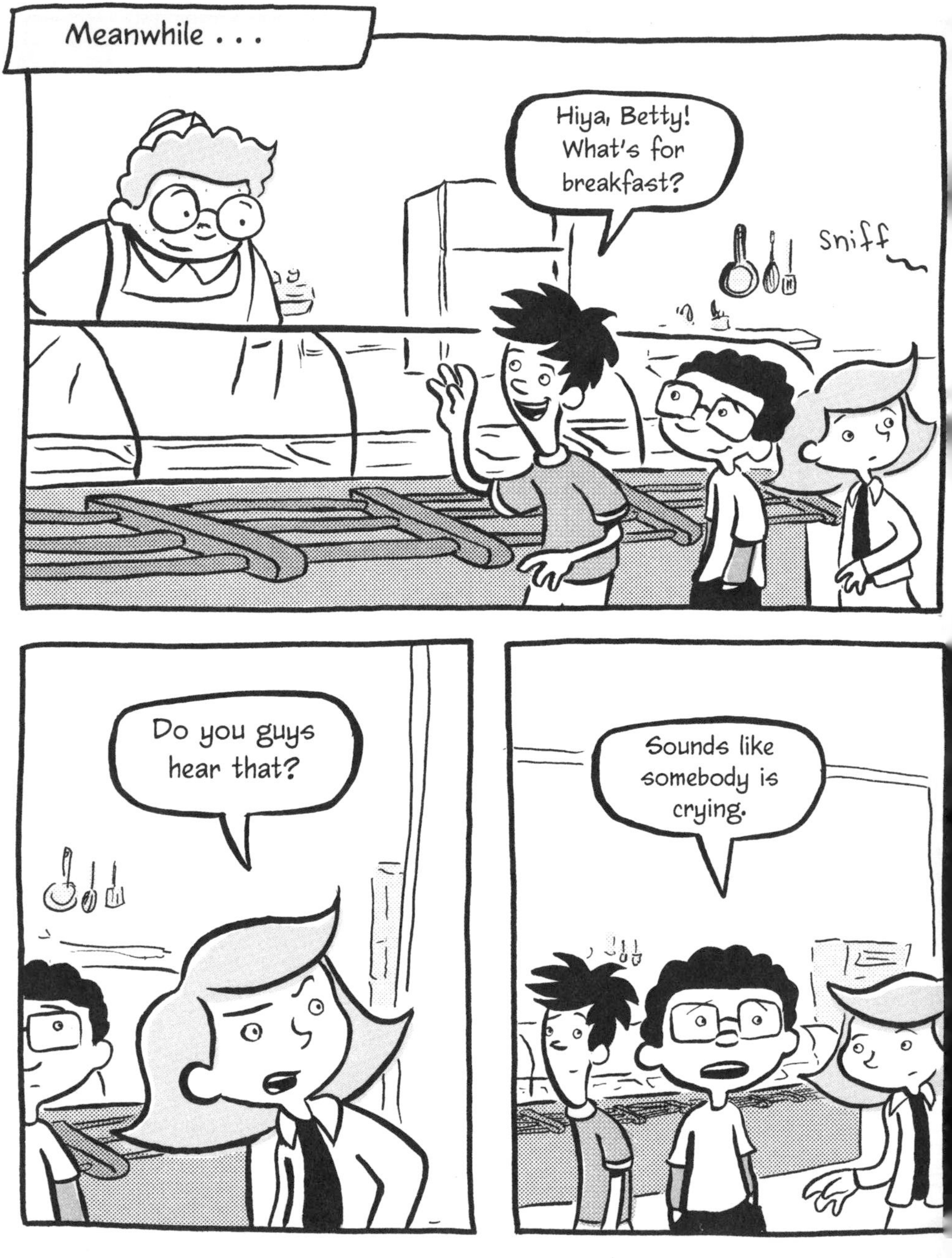
Meanwhile . . .
Hiya, Betty! What's for breakfast?
Sniff
Do you guys hear that?
Sounds like somebody is crying.

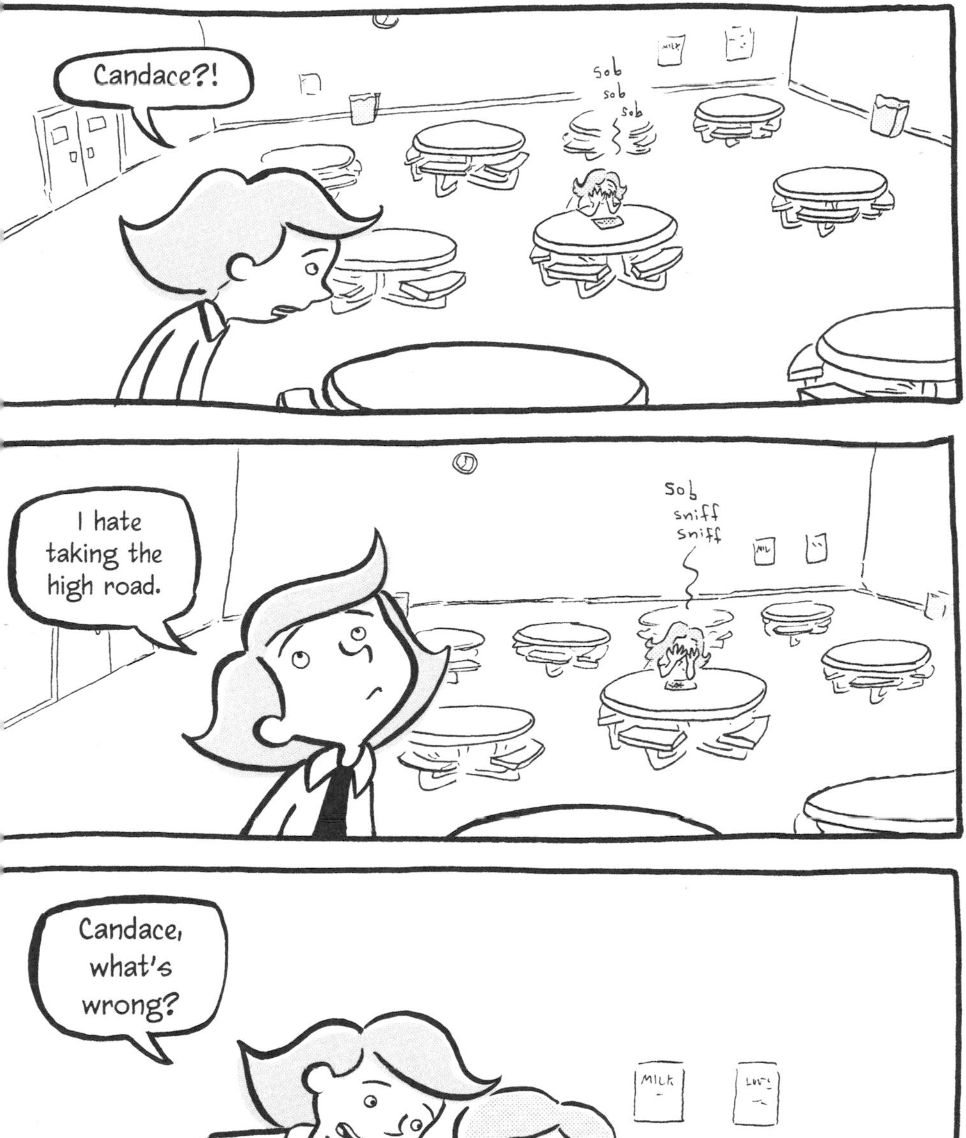
Candace?!
sob
sob
sob
I hate taking the high road.
Sob
sniff
sniff
Candace, what's wrong?
MILK

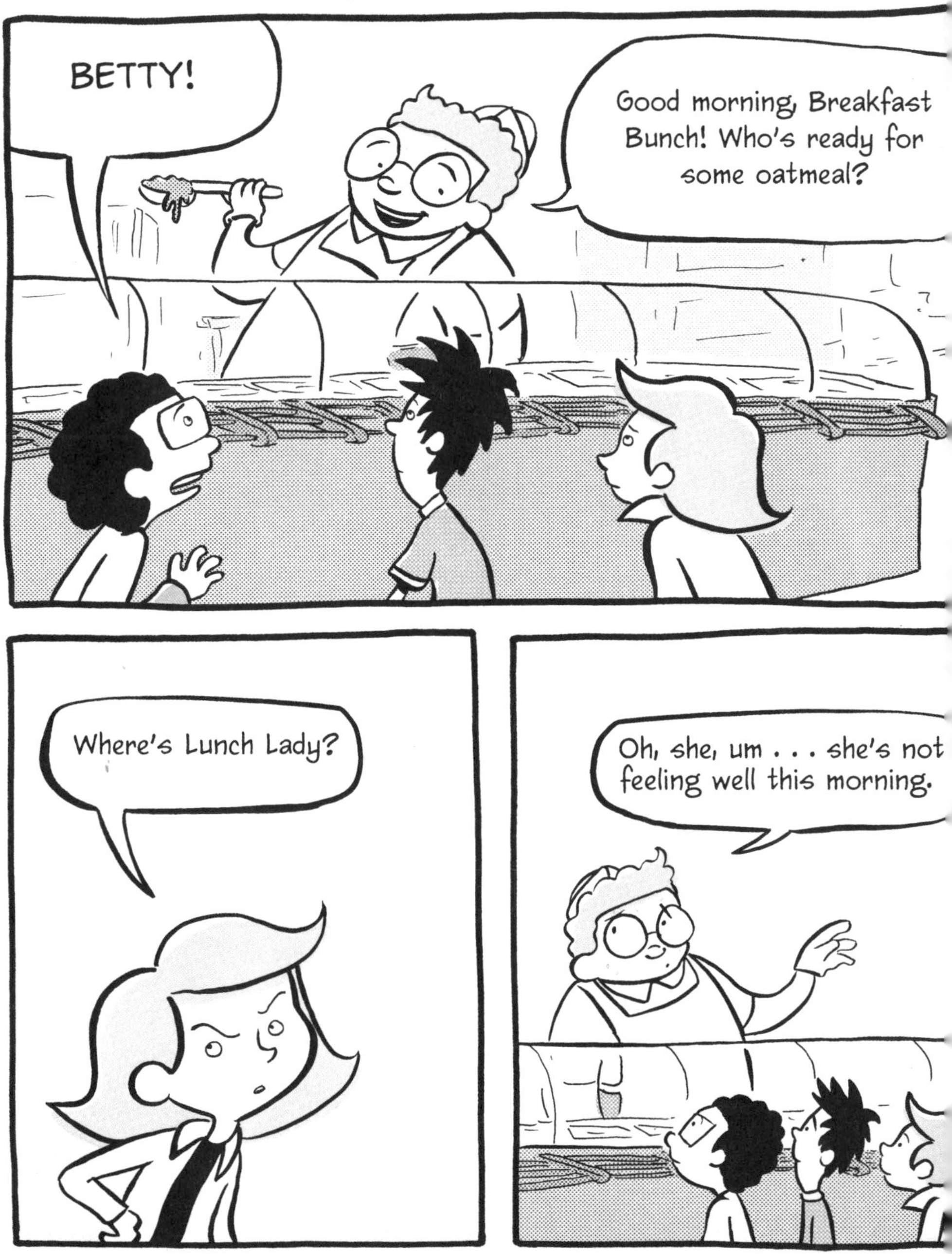
BETTY!
Good morning, Breakfast Bunch! Who's ready for some oatmeal?
Where's Lunch Lady?
Oh, she, um . . . she's not feeling well this morning.

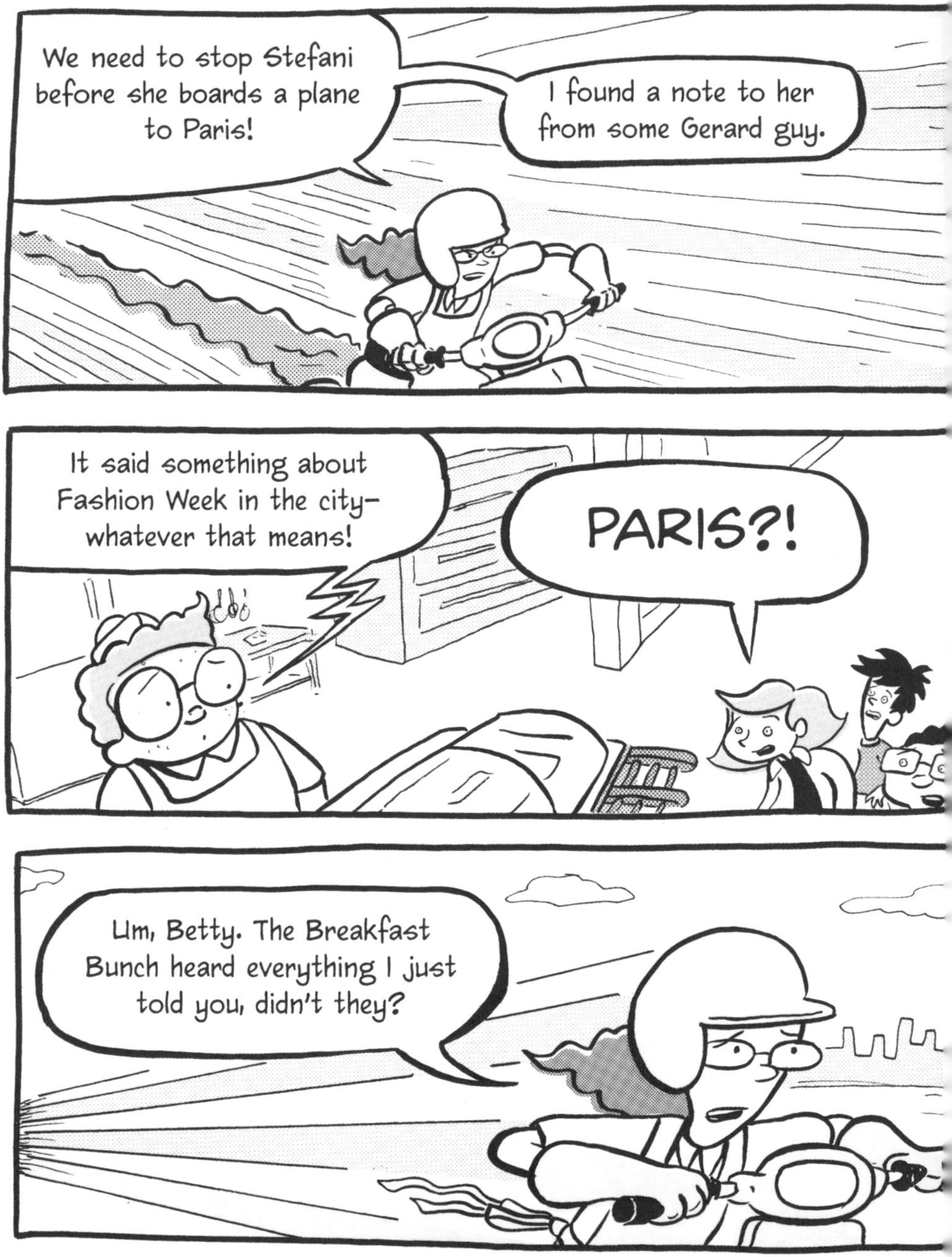

We need to stop Stefani before she boards a plane to Paris!
I found a note to her from some Gerard guy.
It said something about Fashion Week in the city—whatever that means!
PARIS?!
Um, Betty. The Breakfast Bunch heard everything I just told you, didn't they?

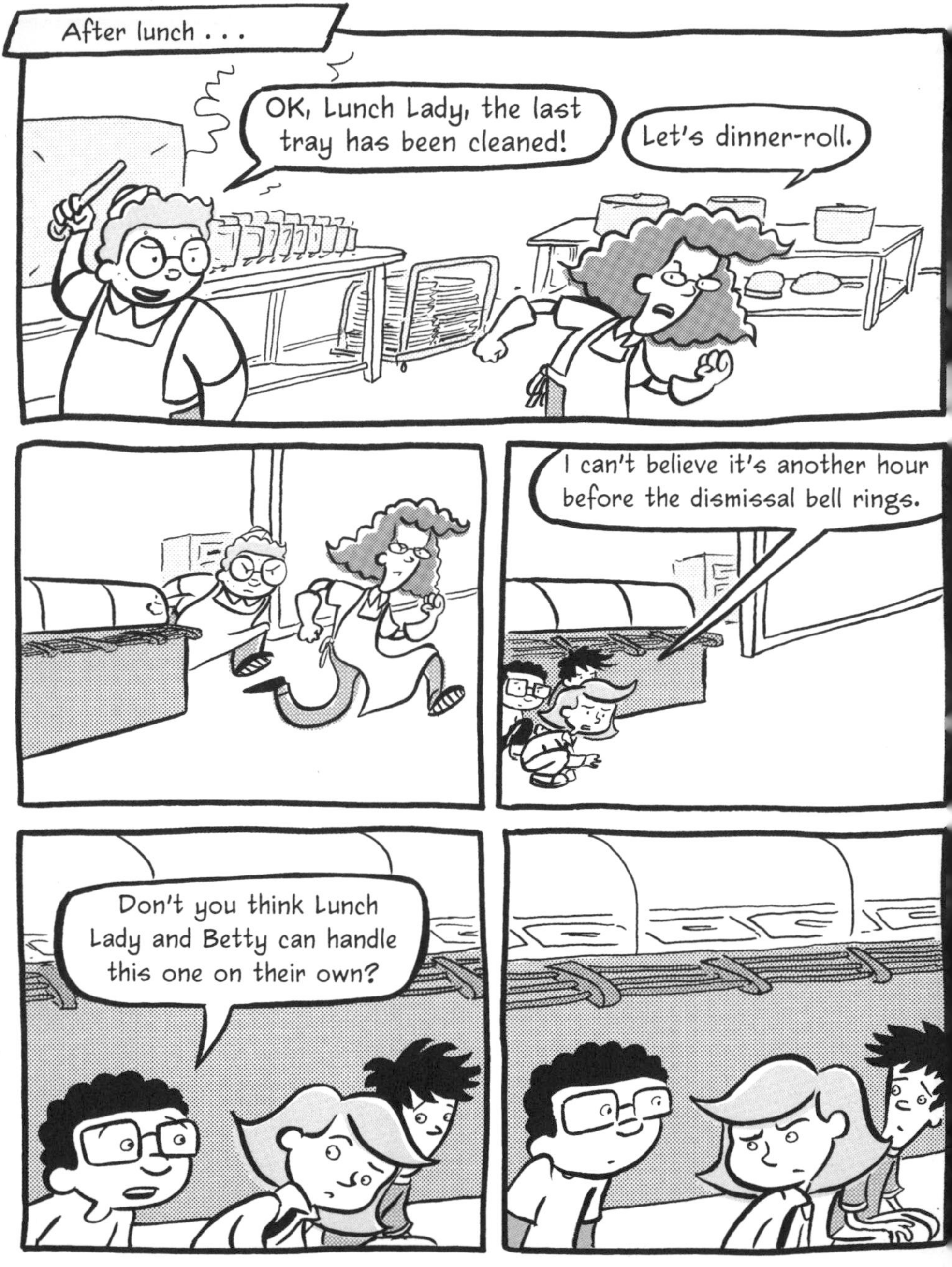
After lunch . . .
OK, Lunch Lady, the last tray has been cleaned!
Let's dinner-roll.
I can't believe it's another hour before the dismissal bell rings.
Don't you think Lunch Lady and Betty can handle this one on their own?

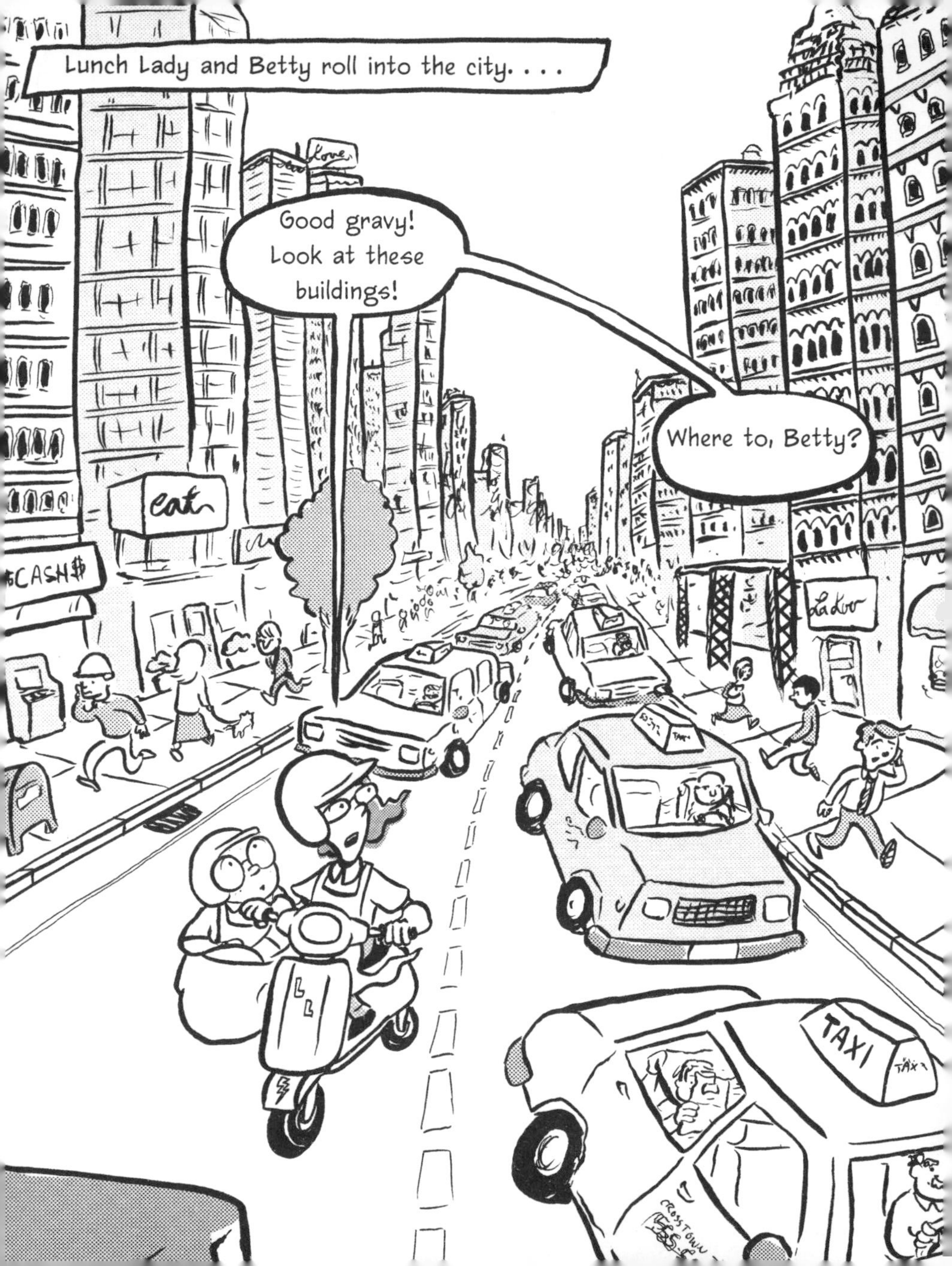
Lunch Lady and Betty roll into the city. . . .
Good gravy! Look at these buildings!
Where to, Betty?
eat
$CASH$
TAXI
CROSSTOWN

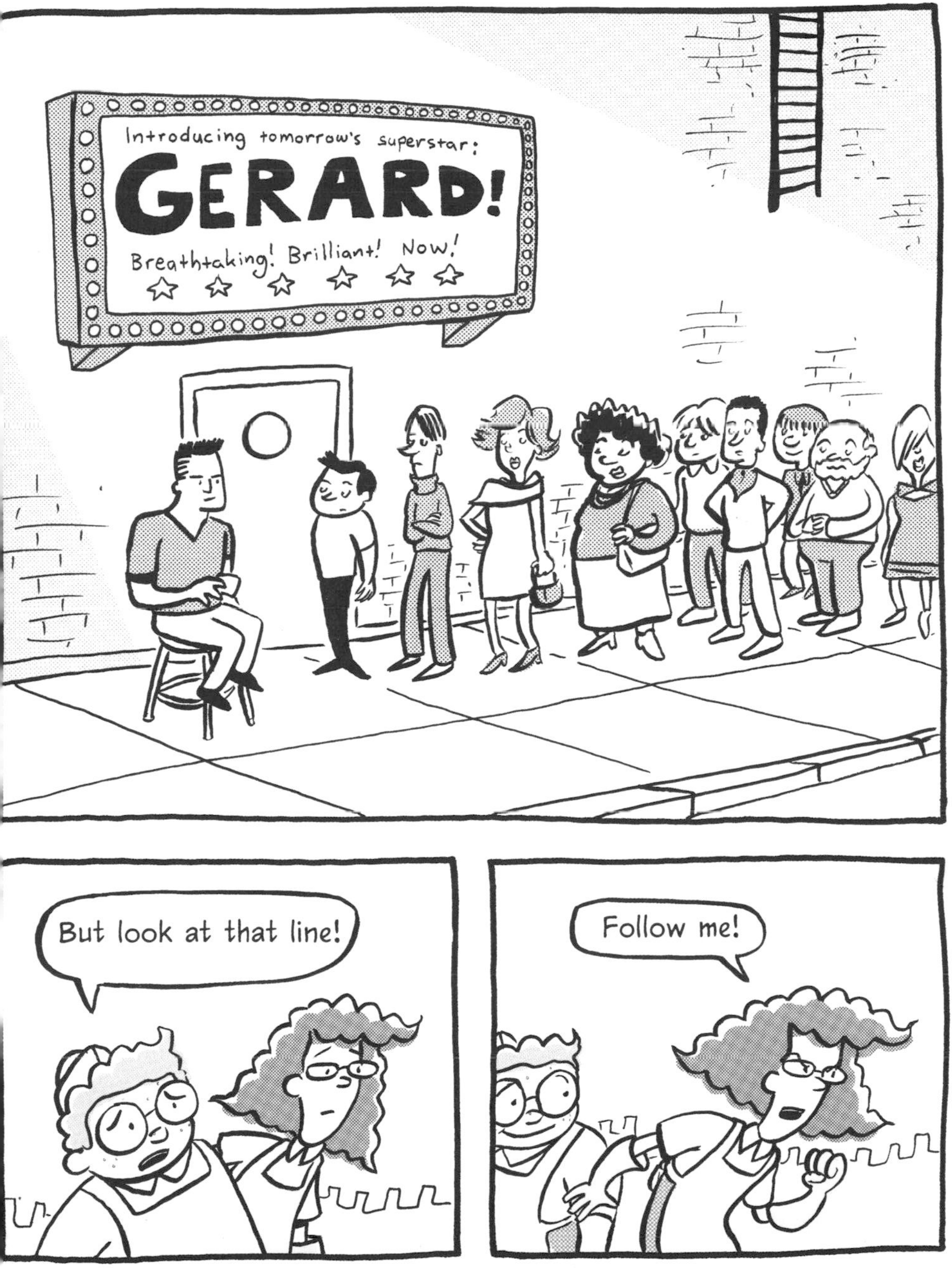
Introducing tomorrow's superstar:
GERARD!
Breathtaking! Brilliant! Now!
But look at that line!
Follow me!

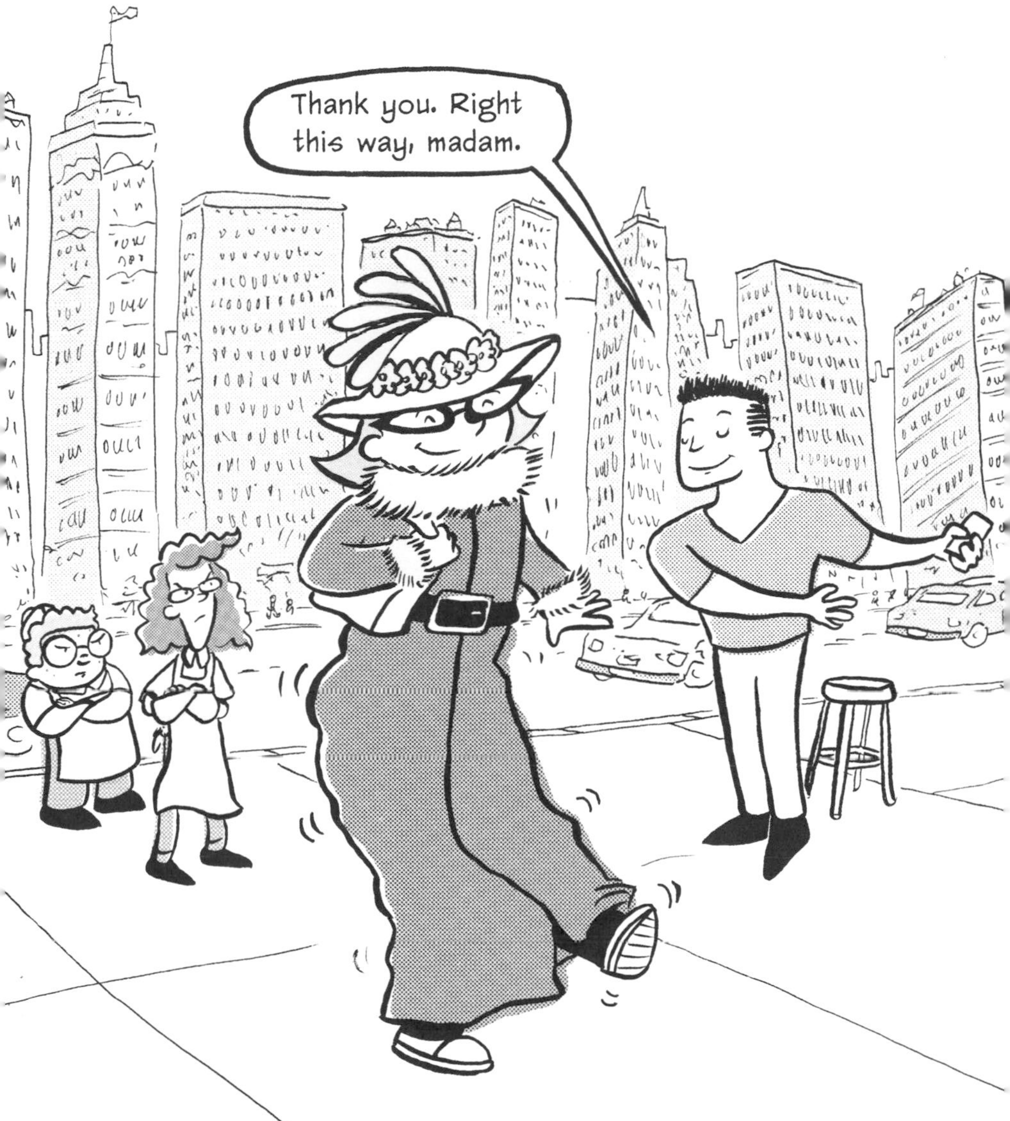
Thank you. Right this way, madam.

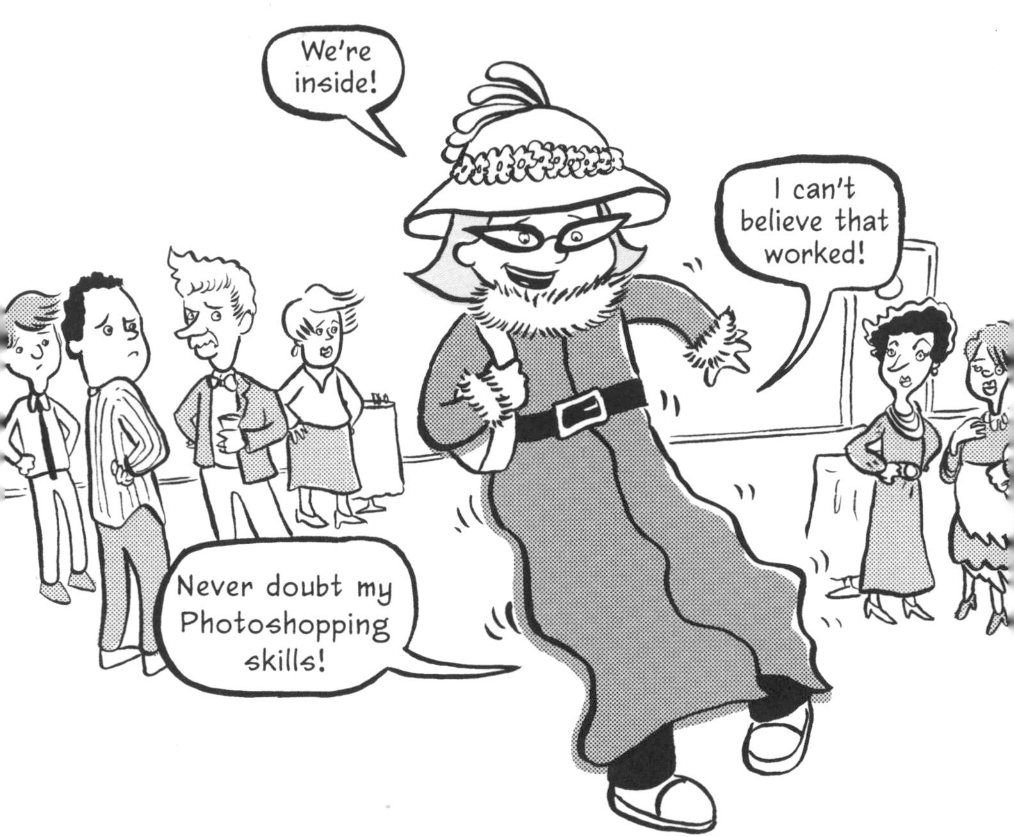
We're inside!
I can't believe that worked!
Never doubt my Photoshopping skills!

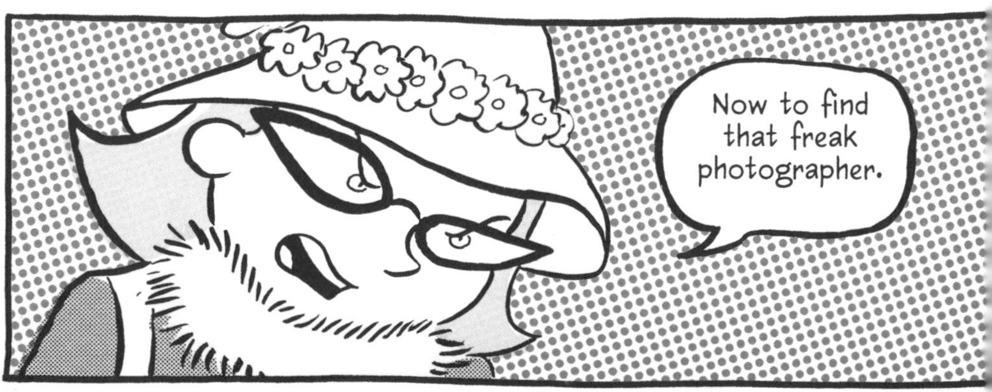
Now to find that freak photographer.

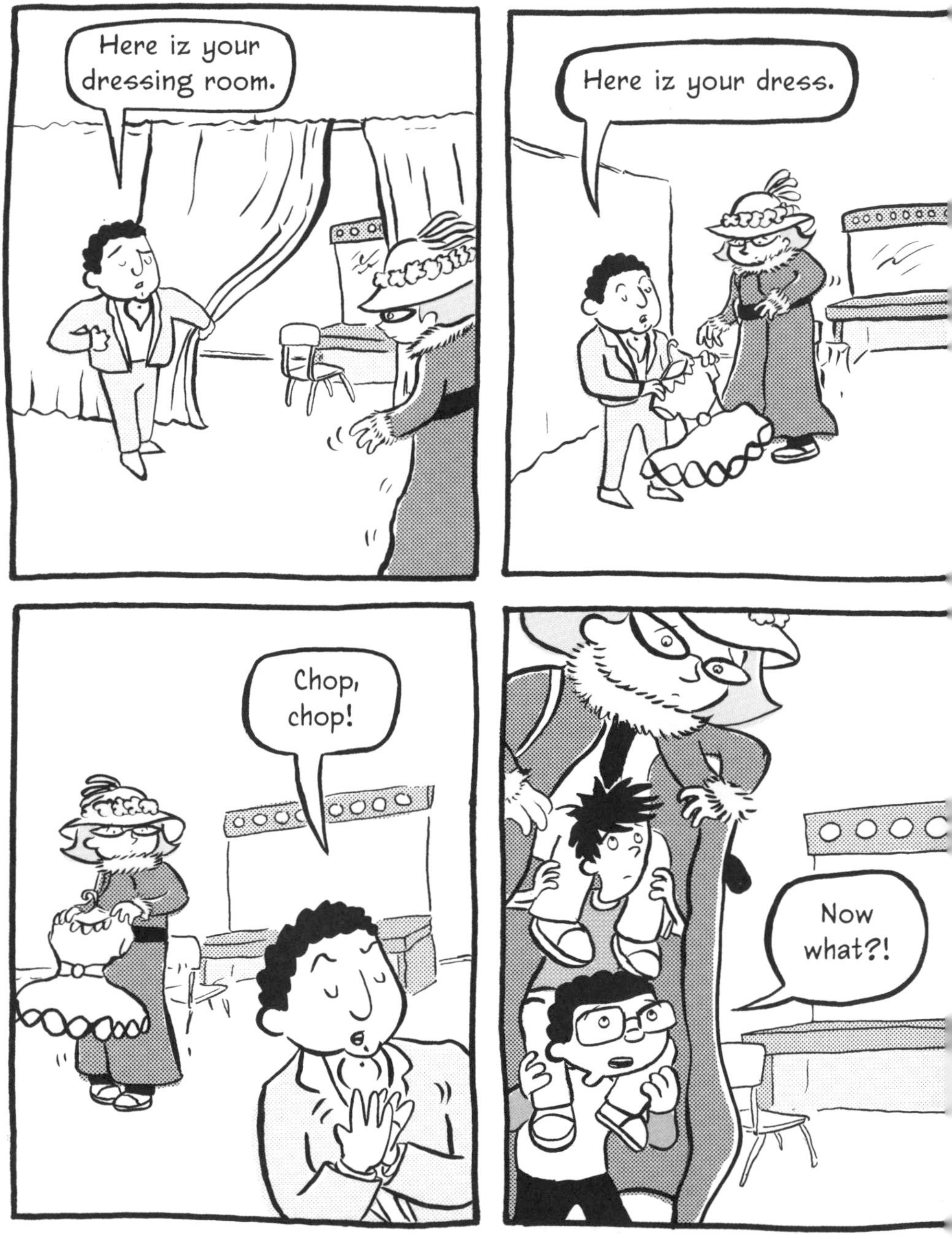
Here iz your dressing room.
Here iz your dress.
Chop, chop!
Now what?!

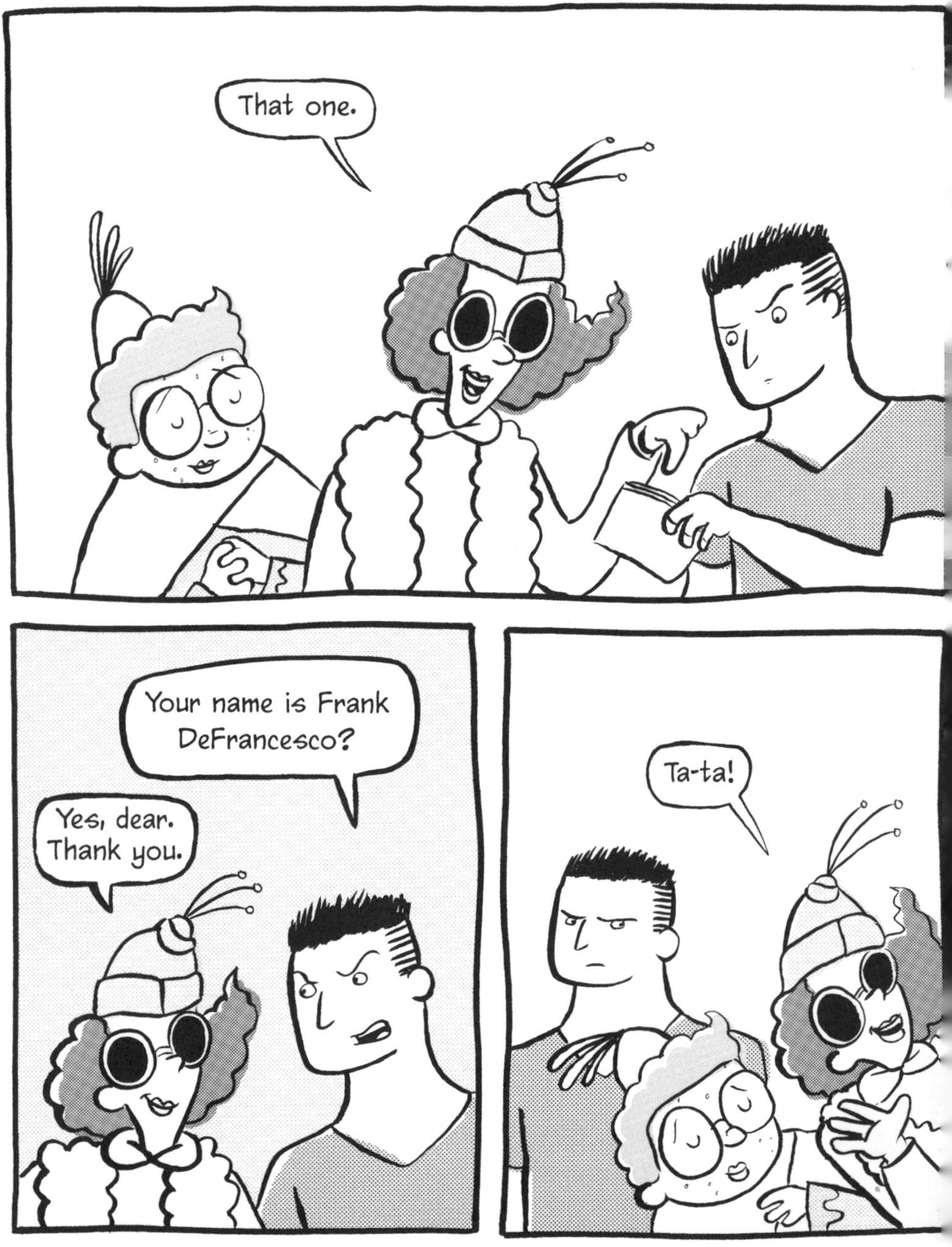
That one.
Your name is Frank DeFrancesco?
Yes, dear. Thank you.
Ta-ta!

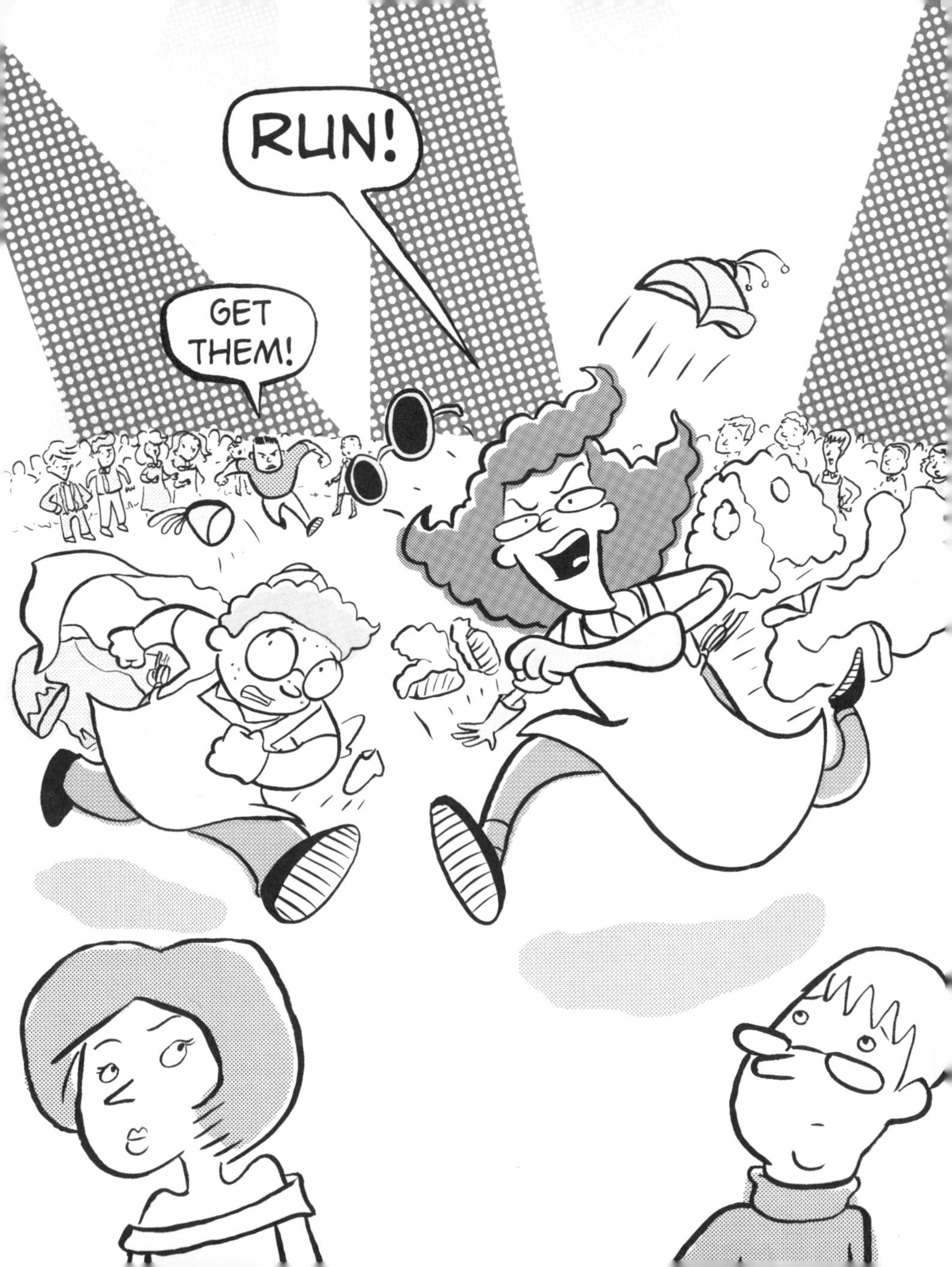
RUN!
GET THEM!

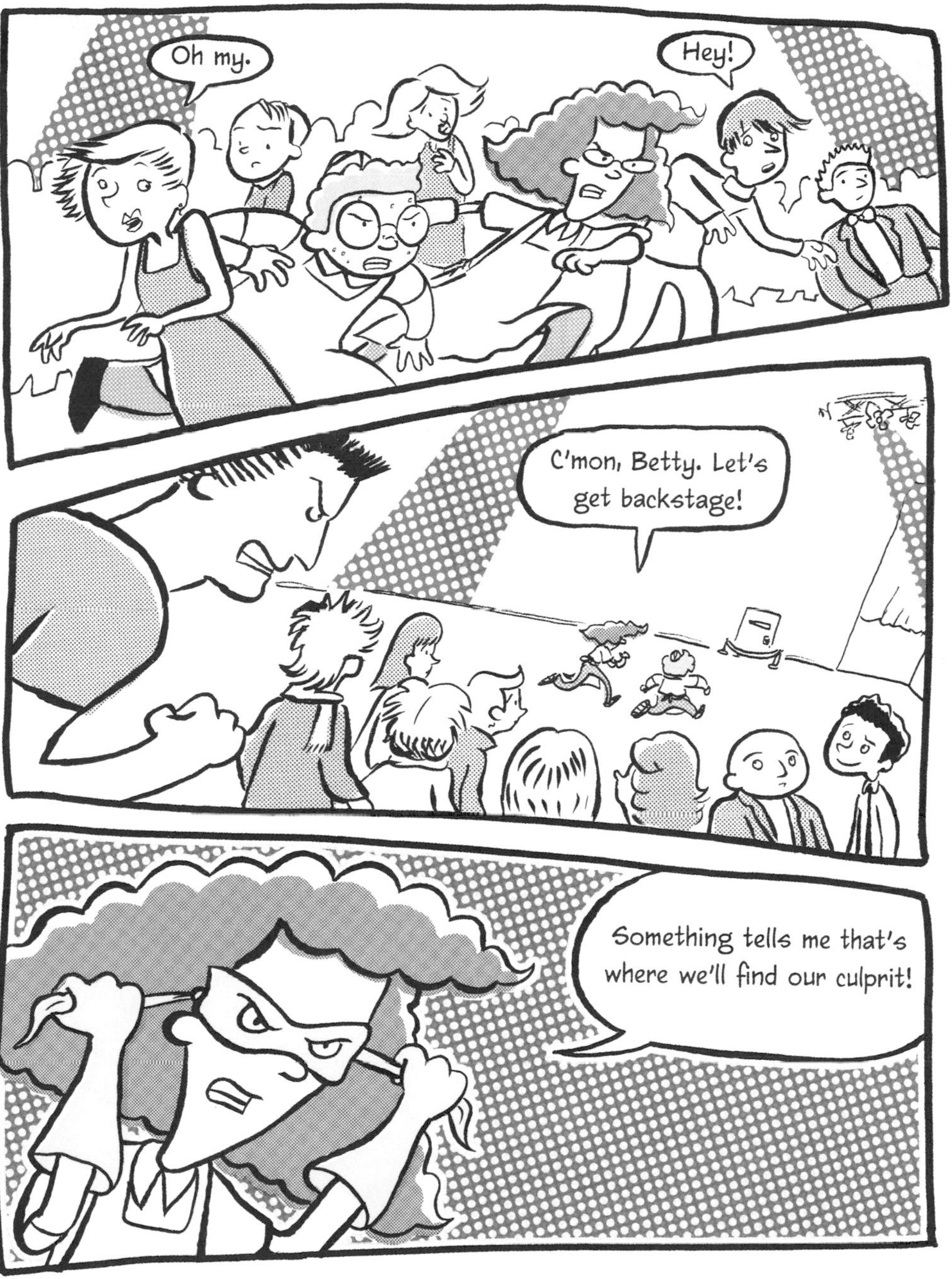
Oh my.
Hey!
C'mon, Betty. Let's get backstage!
Something tells me that's where we'll find our culprit!

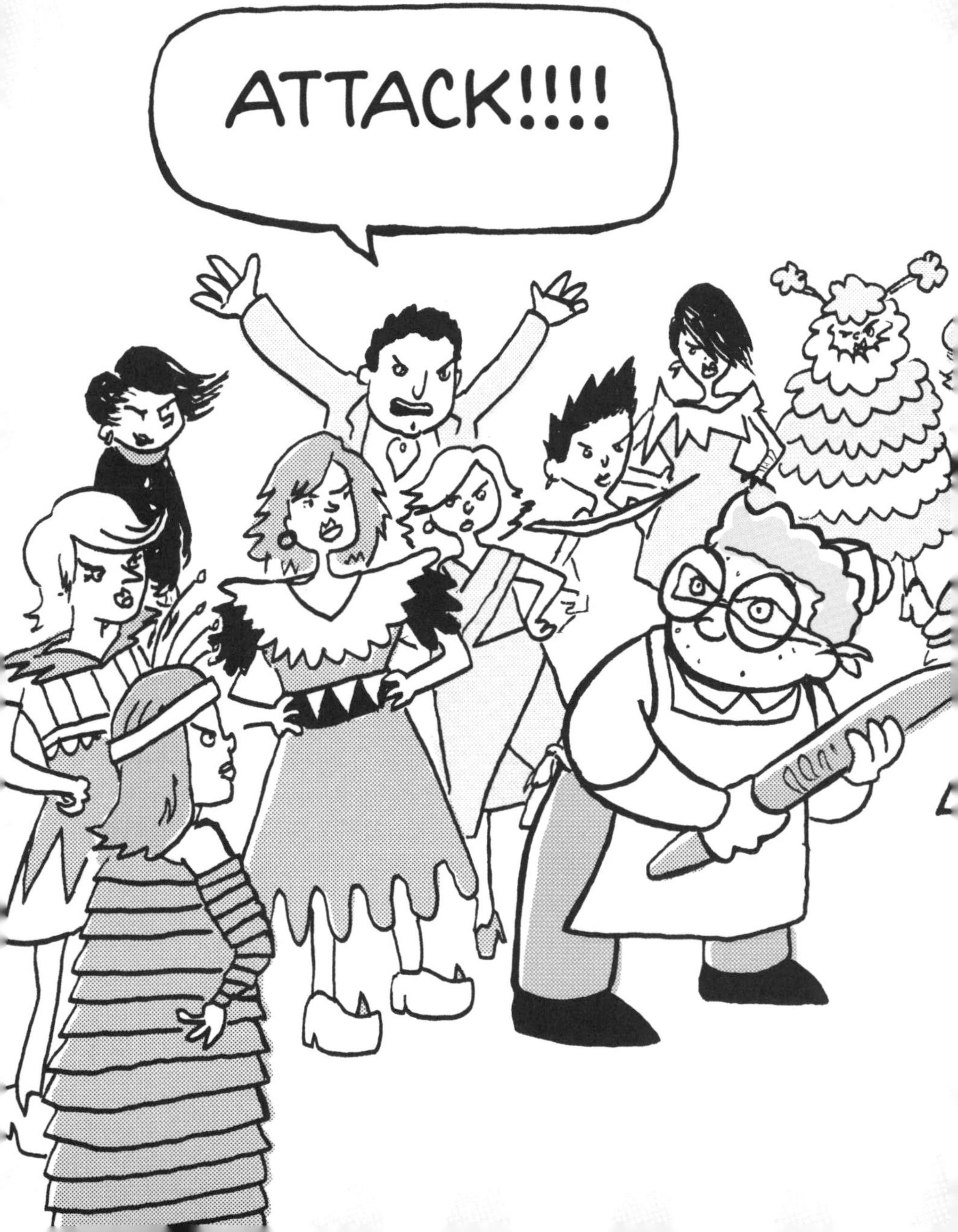
ATTACK!!!!

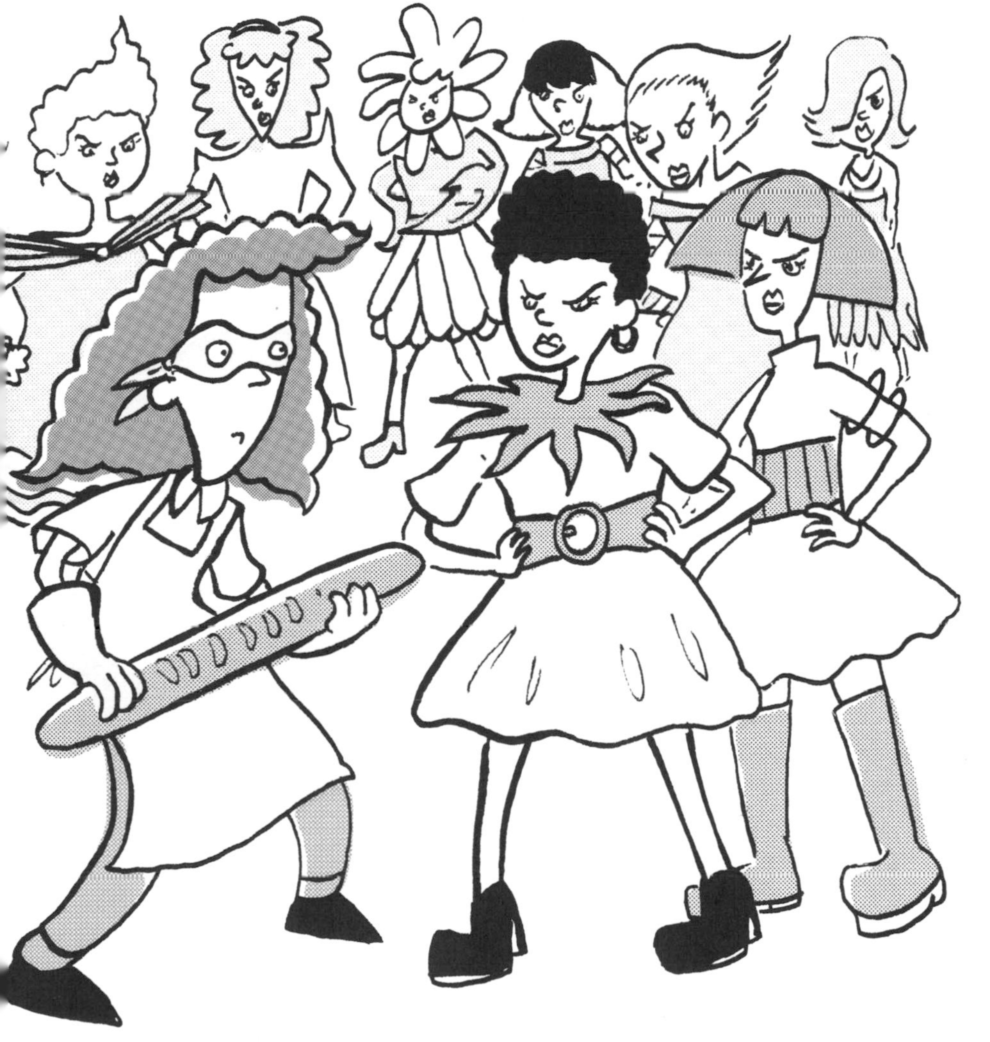

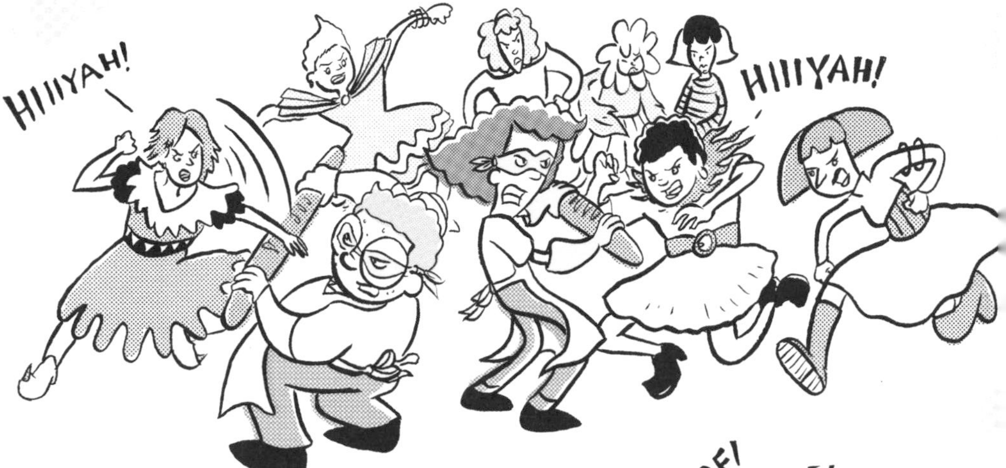
HIIIYAH!
HIIIYAH!

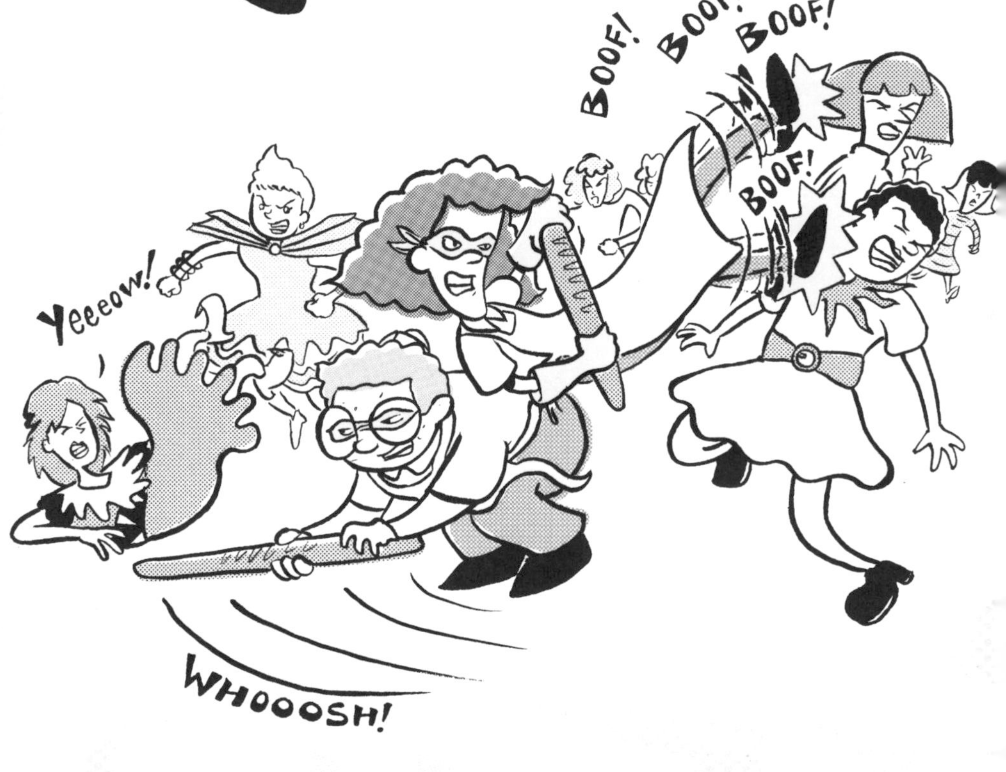
BOOF!
BOOF!
BOOF!
Yeeeow!
BOOF!
WHOOOSH!

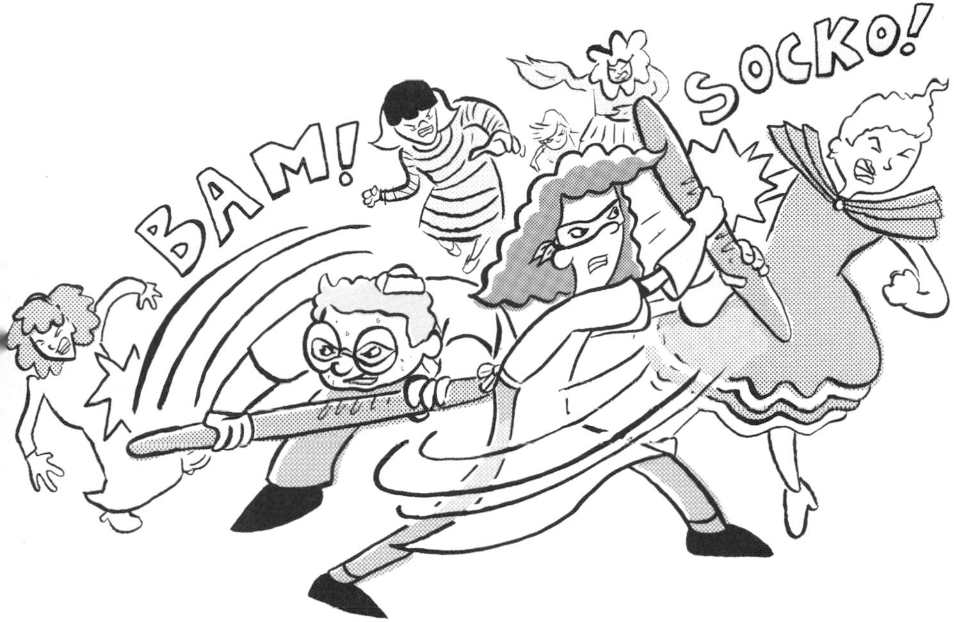
BAM!
SOCKO!

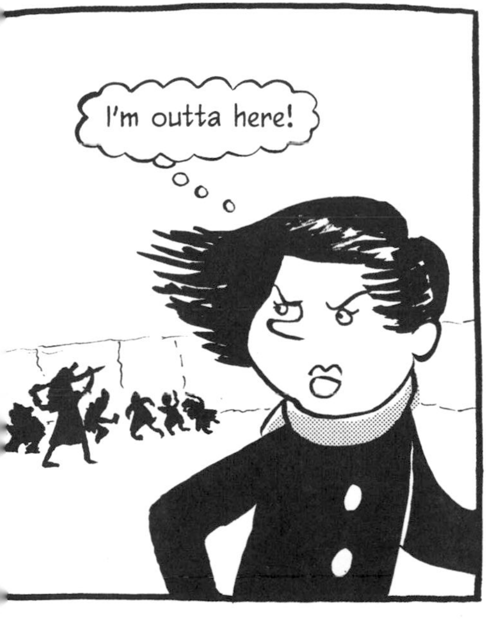
I'm outta here!

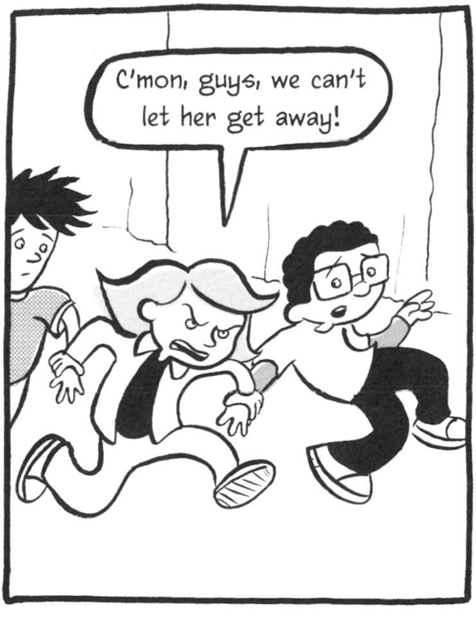
C'mon, guys, we can't let her get away!

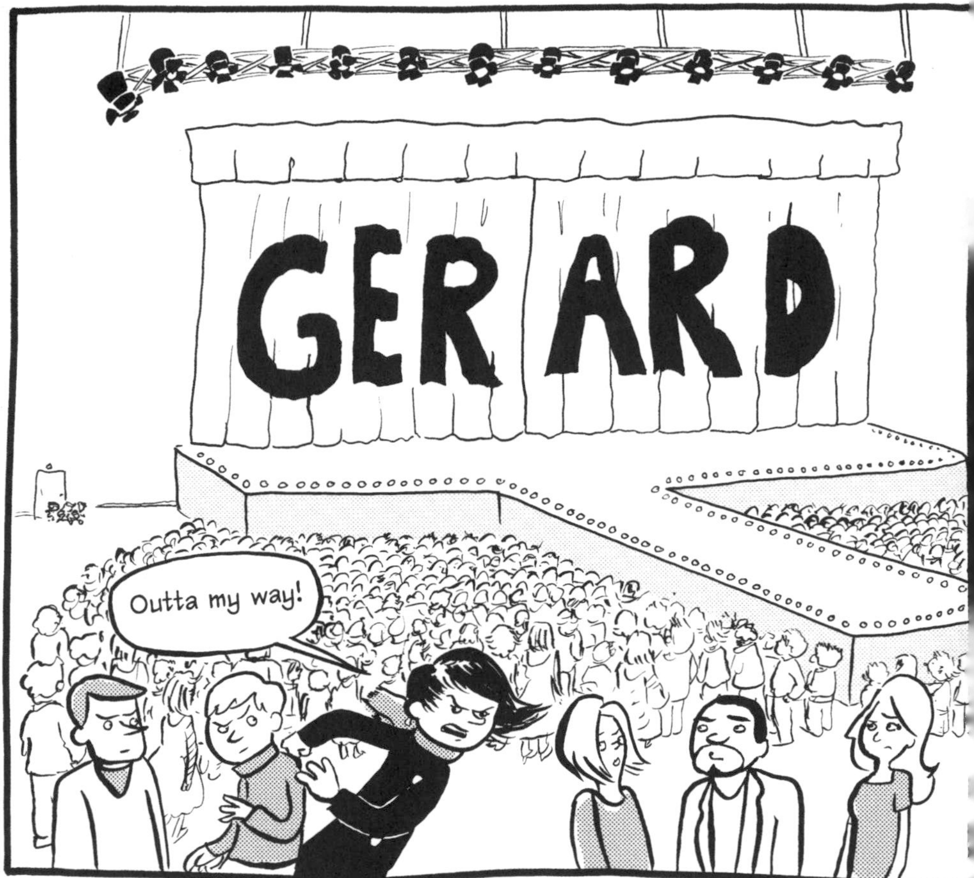
GERARD
Outta my way!

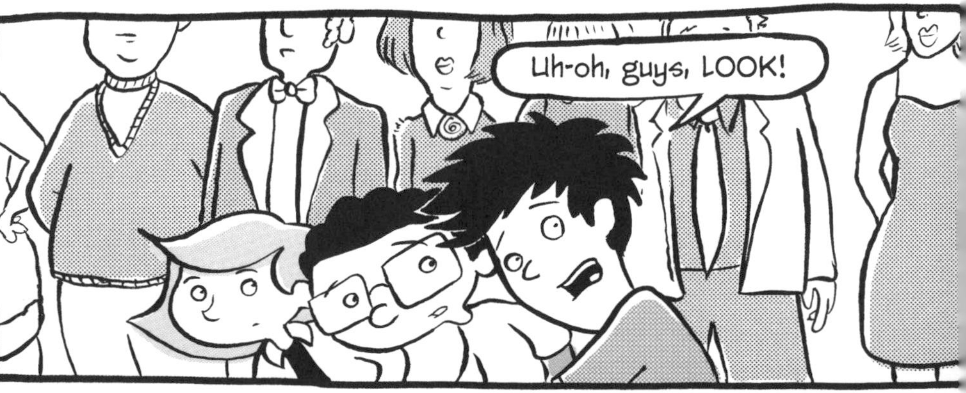
Uh-oh, guys, LOOK!

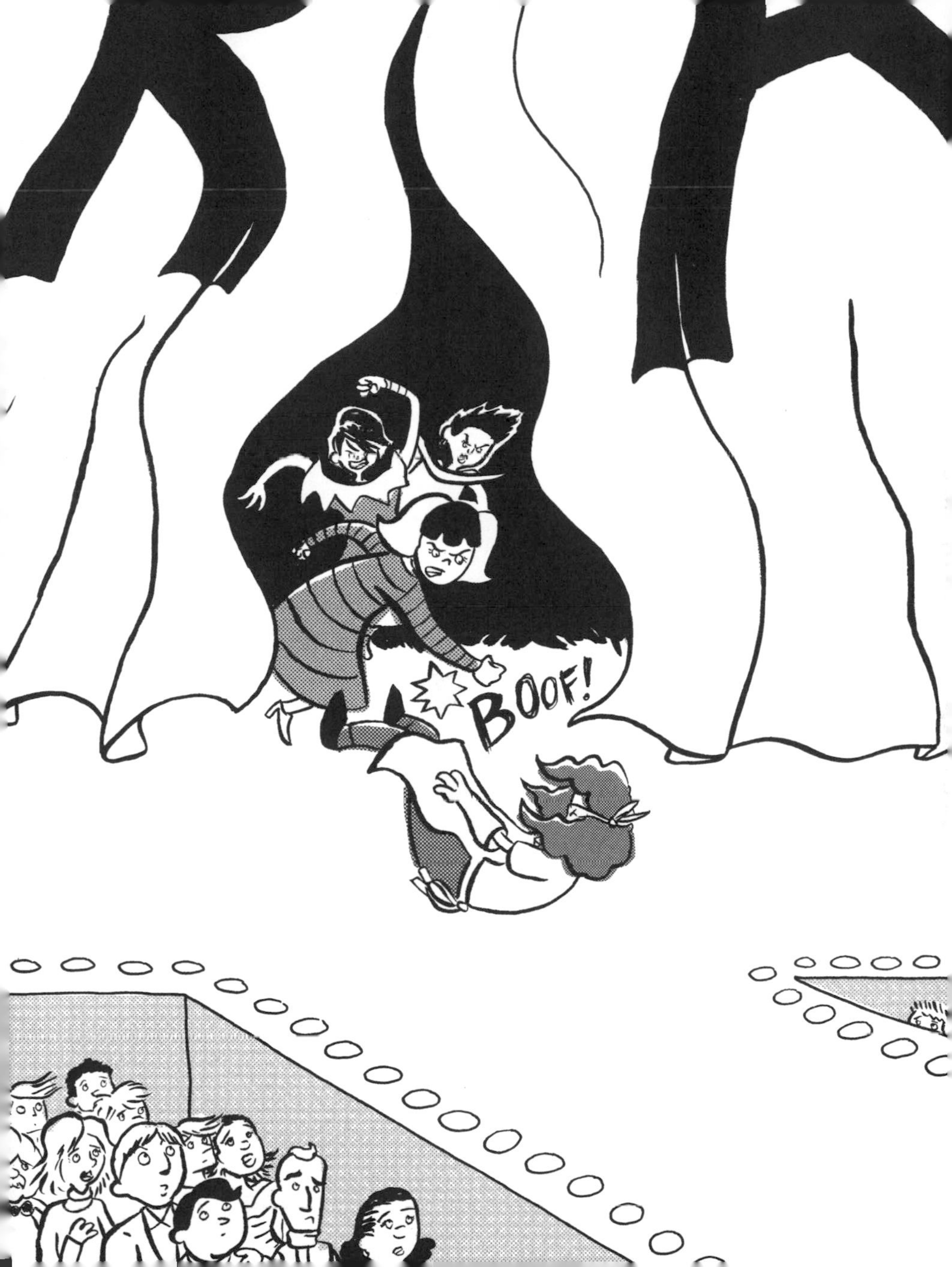
BOOF!

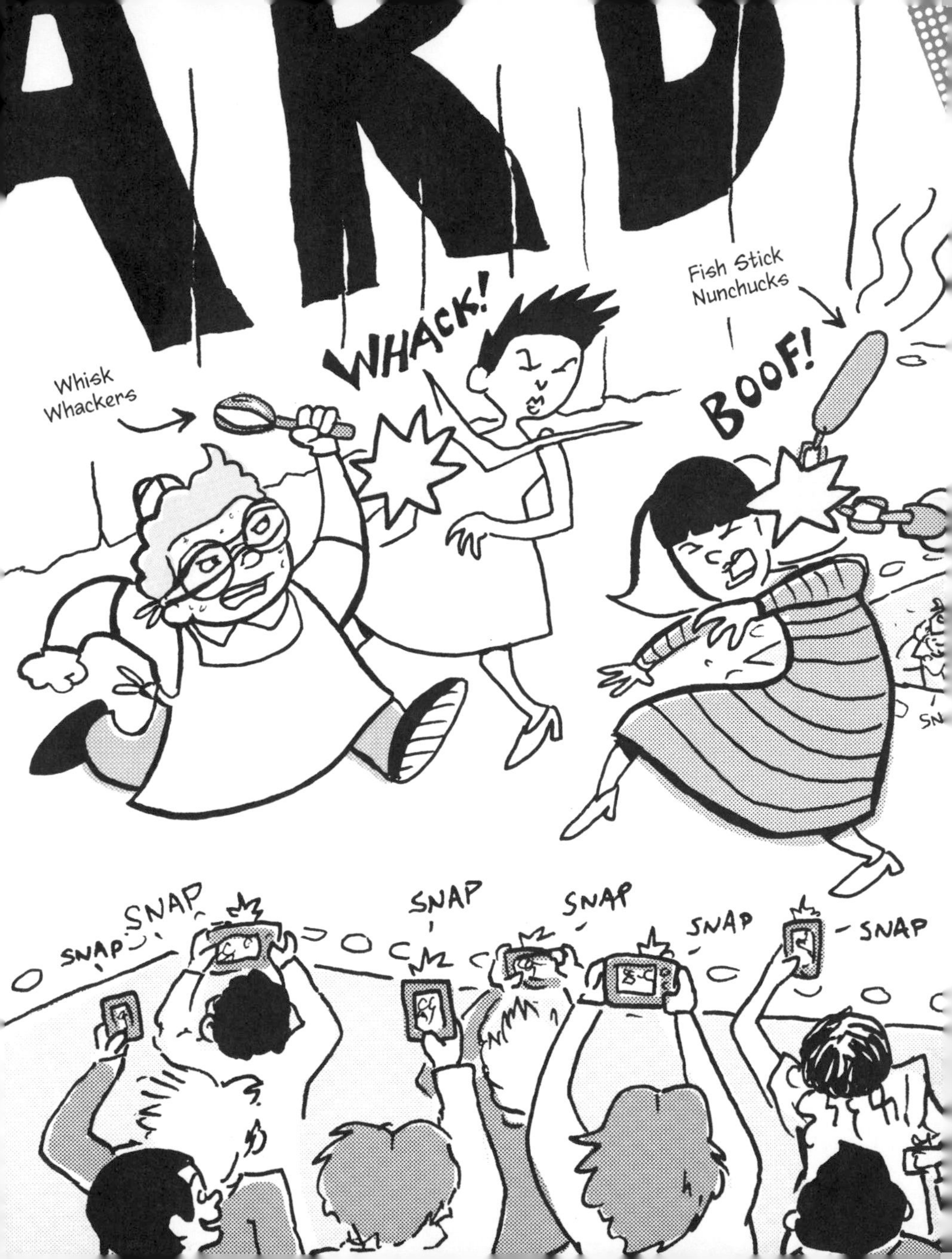
Whisk Whackers
WHACK!
Fish Stick Nunchucks
BOOF!
SNAP
SNAP
SNAP
SNAP
SNAP
SNAP

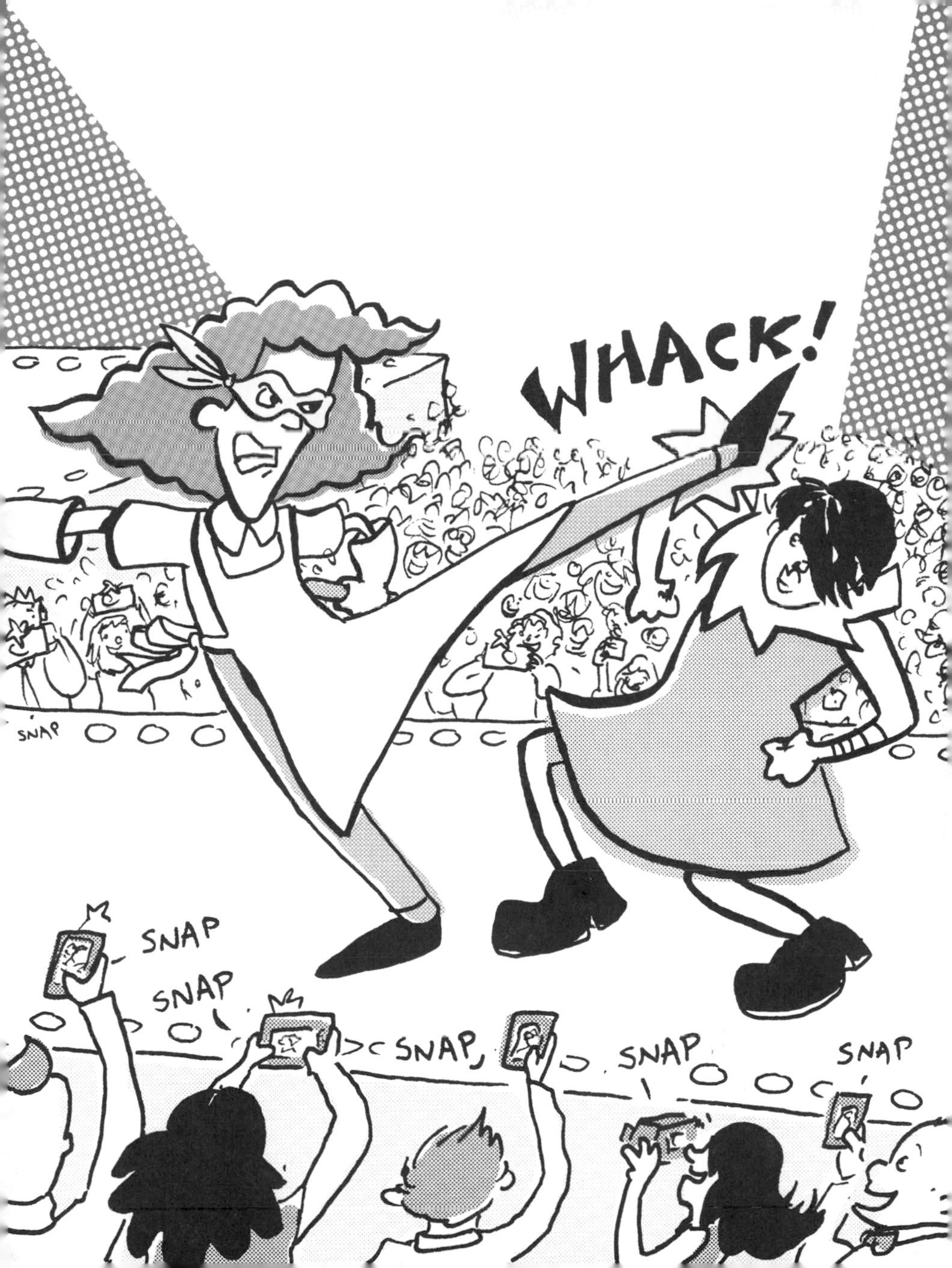
WHACK!
SNAP
SNAP
SNAP
SNAP,
SNAP
SNAP

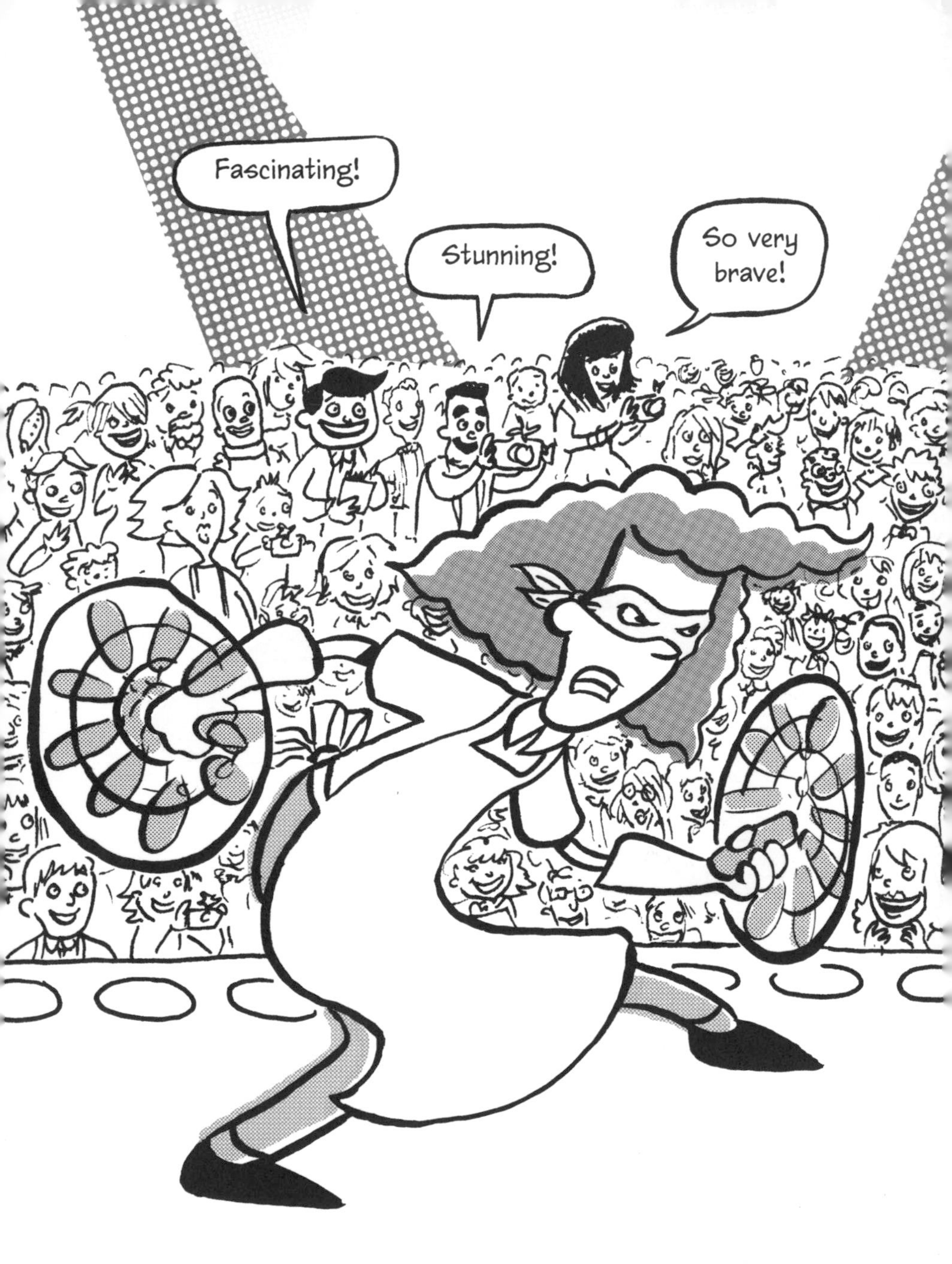
Fascinating!
Stunning!
So very brave!

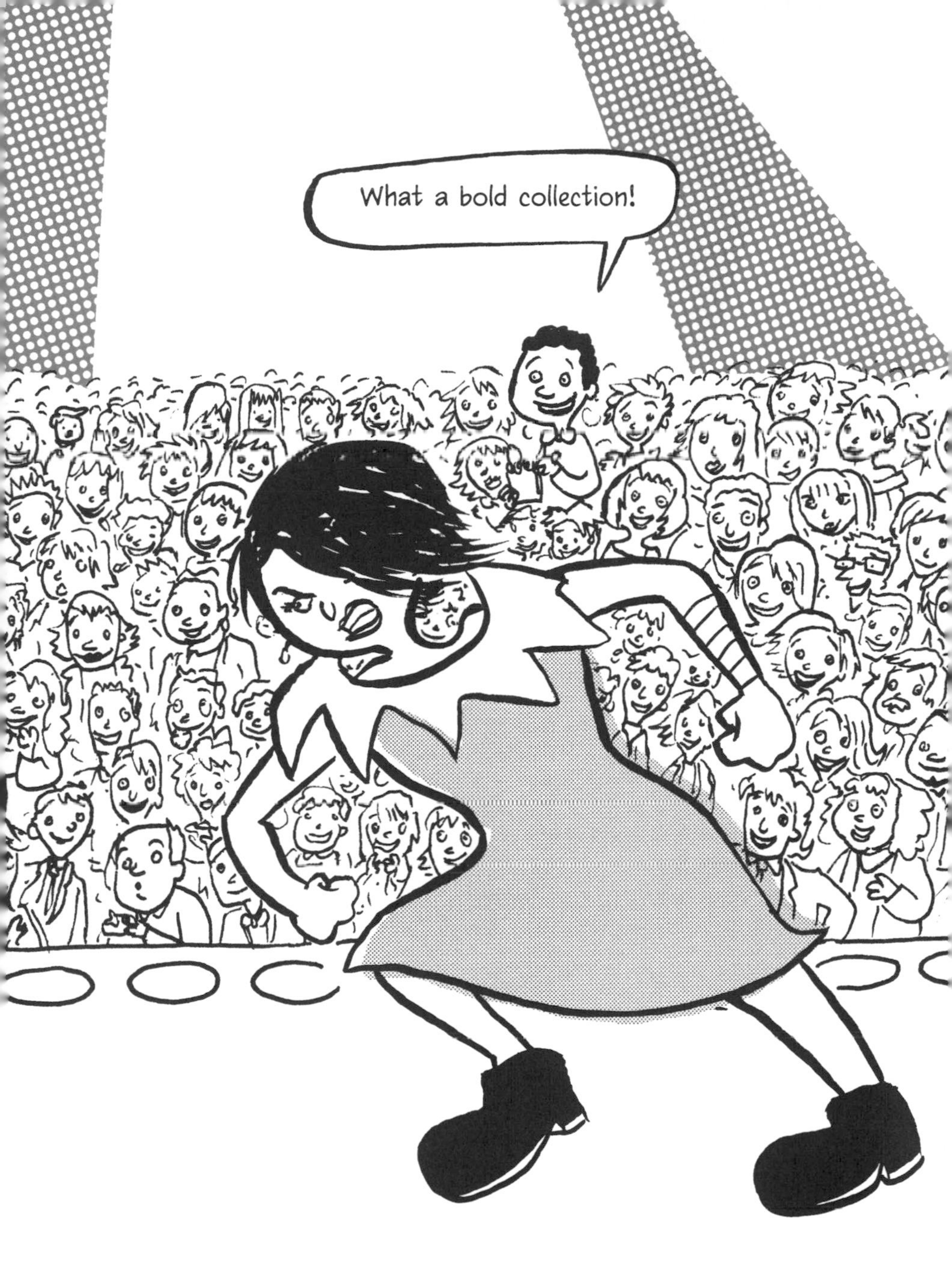
What a bold collection!

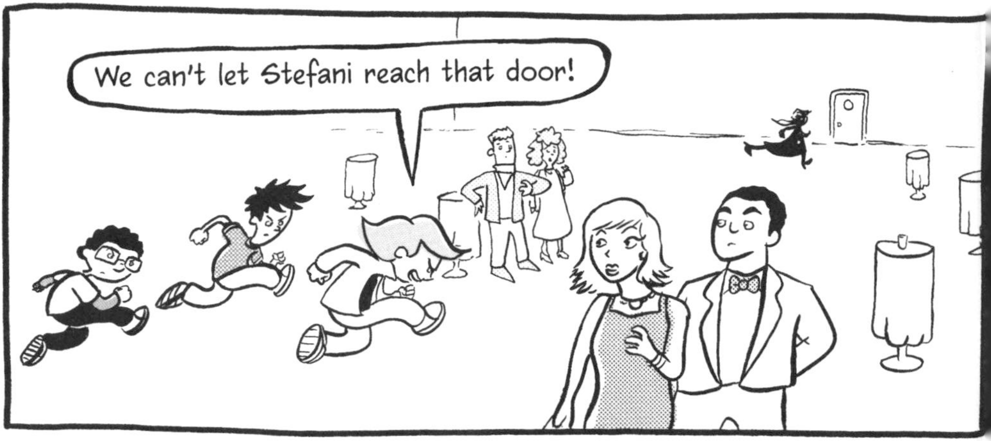
We can't let Stefani reach that door!

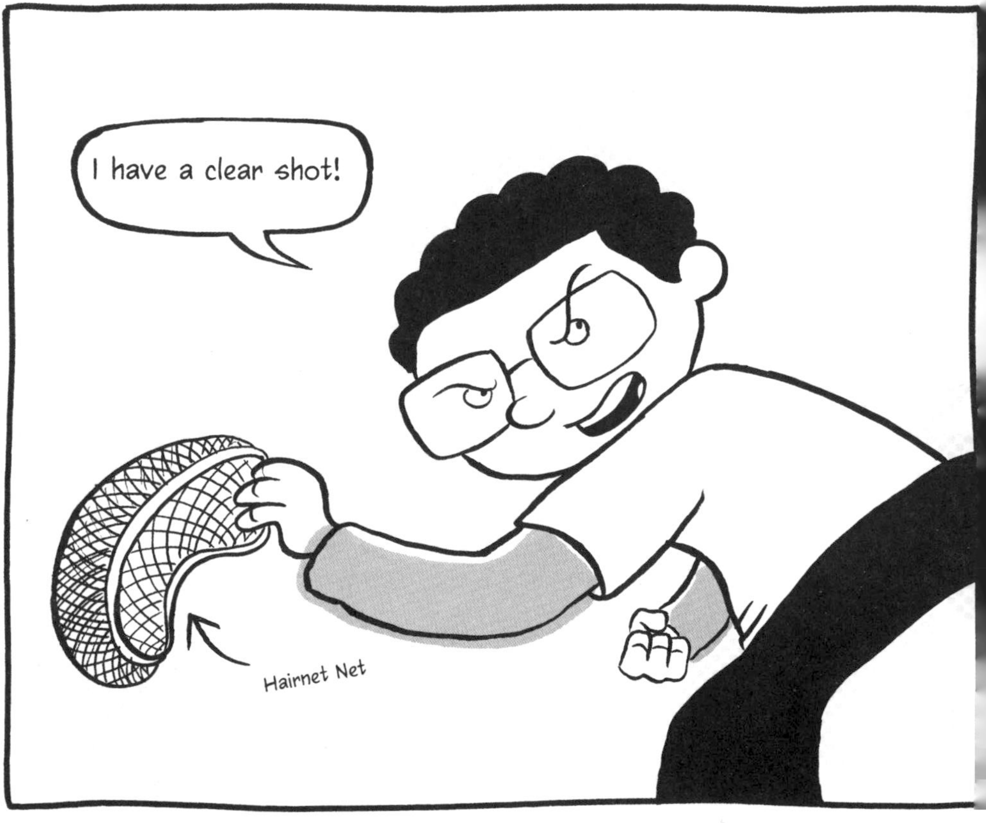
I have a clear shot!
Hairnet Net

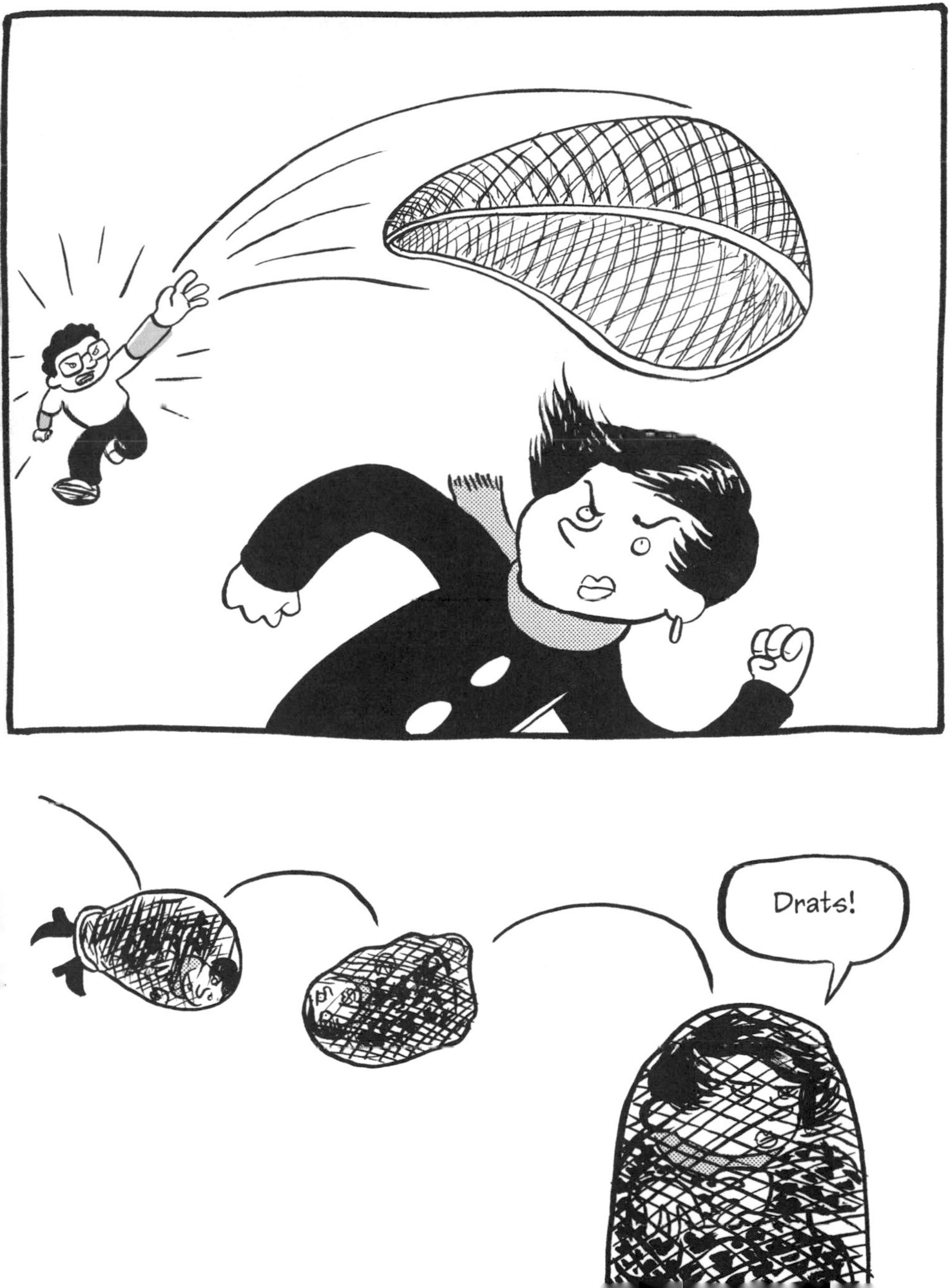
Drats!

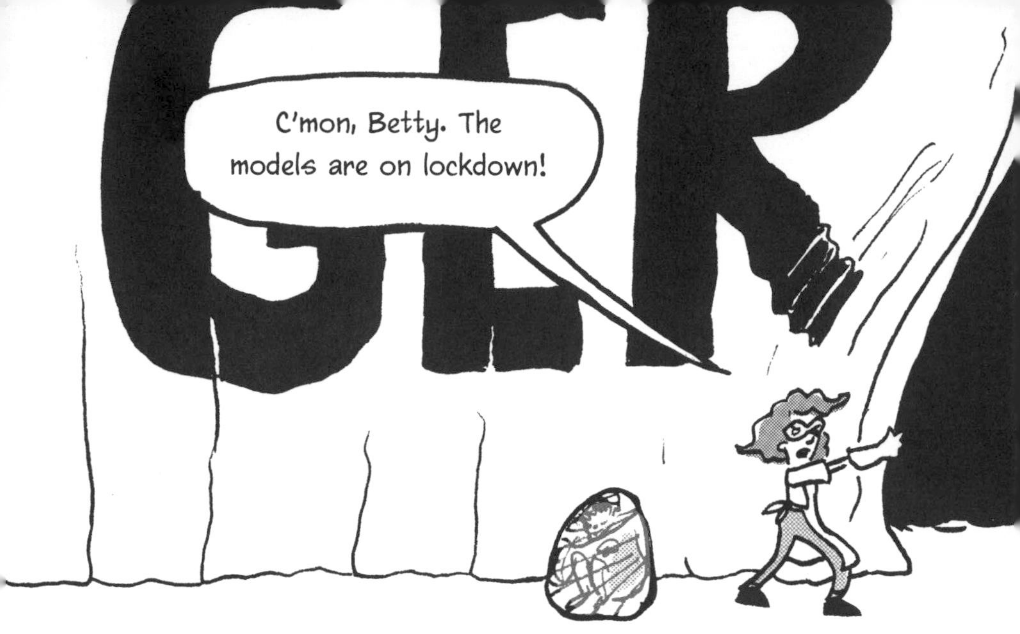
C'mon, Betty. The models are on lockdown!

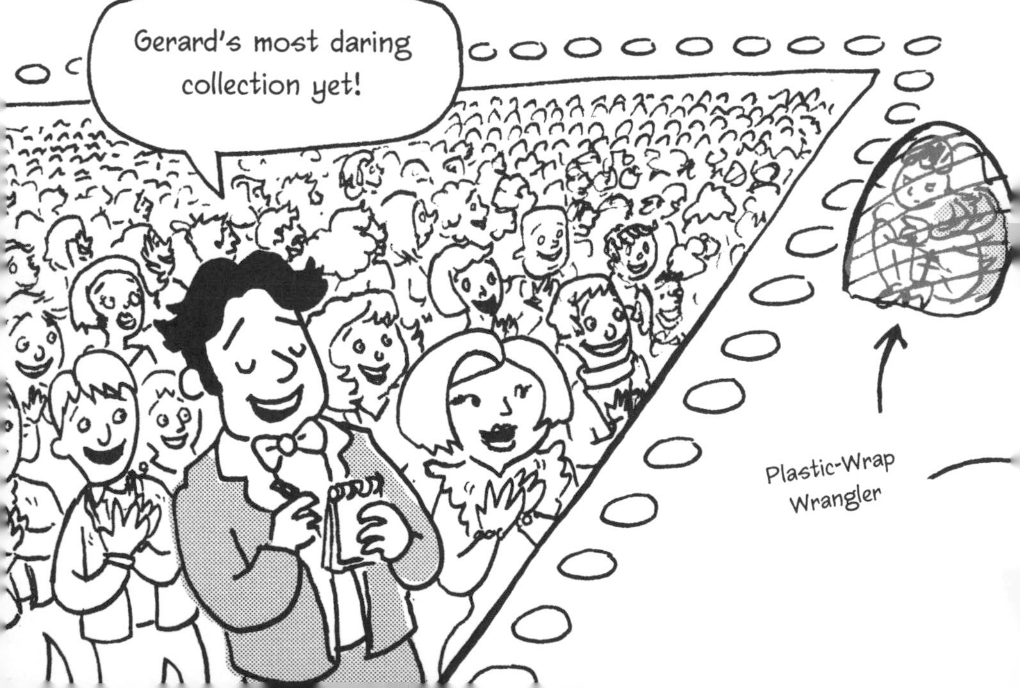
Gerard's most daring collection yet!
Plastic-Wrap Wrangler

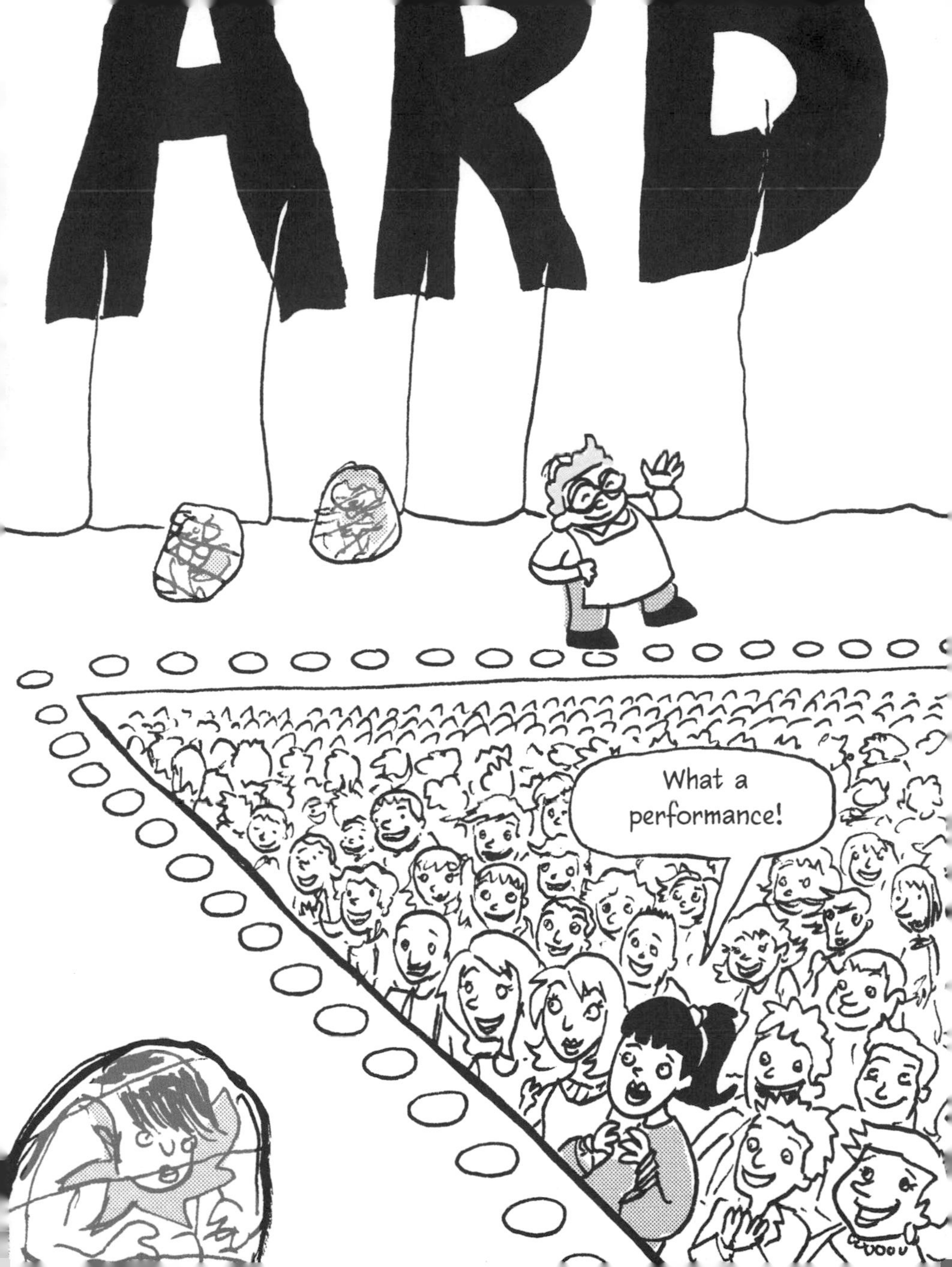
ARD
What a performance!

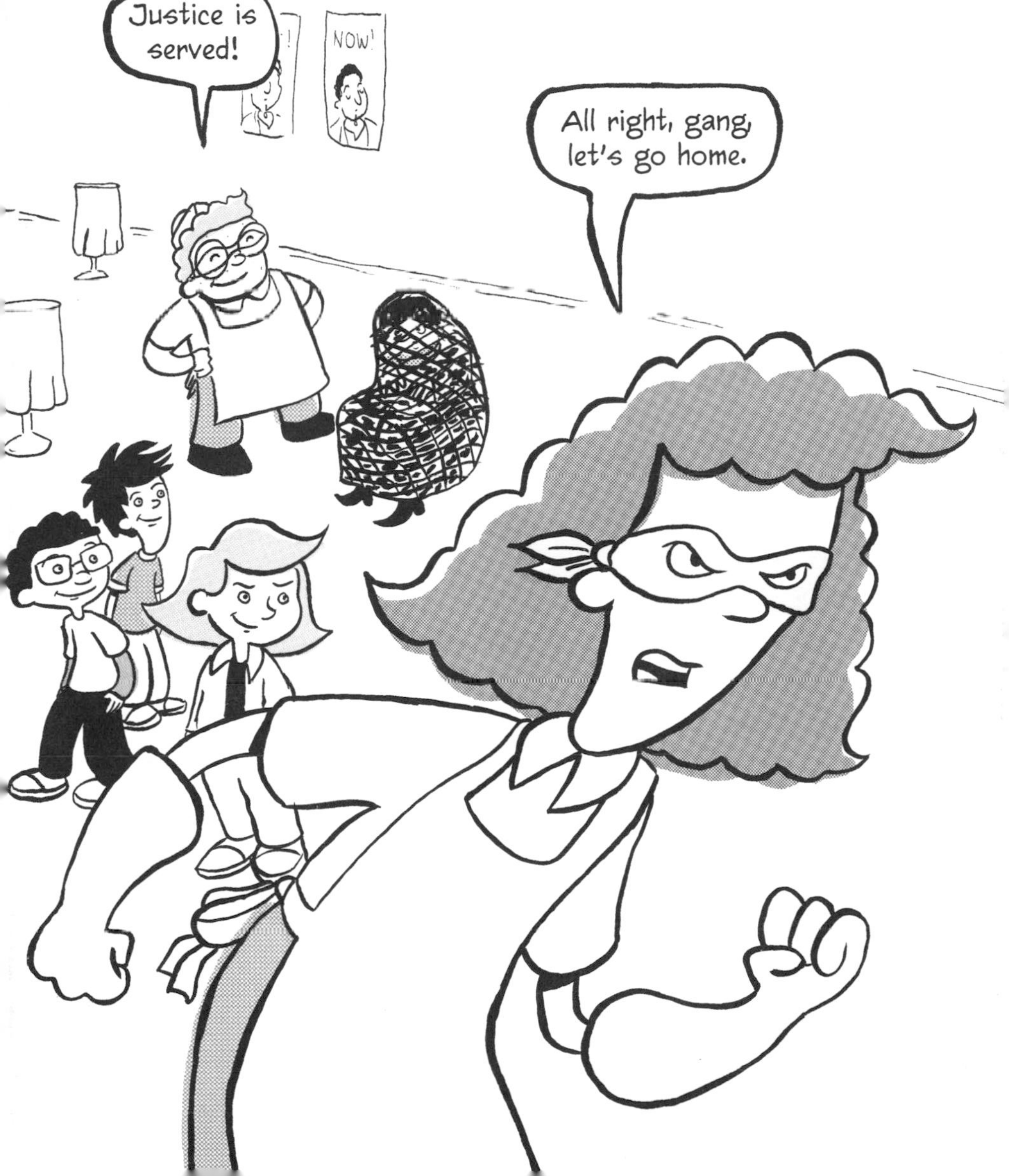
Justice is served!
NOW!
All right, gang, let's go home.

FOR JEANNIE AND BETTY
and all of their years of dedication and service to Gates Lane School

The author would like to acknowledge the color work in this book by Joey Weiser and Michele Chidester.

THIS IS A BORZOI BOOK PUBLISHED BY ALFRED A. KNOPF

Visit us on the Web! randomhouse.com/kids

Educators and librarians, for a variety of teaching tools, visit us at RHTeachersLibrarians.com

Library of Congress Cataloging-in-Publication Data
Krosoczka, Jarrett.
Lunch lady and the picture day peril / Jarrett J. Krosoczka. — 1st ed.
p.   cm. — (Lunch lady ; [8])
Summary: When eccentric photographer Stefani DePino comes to Thompson Brook to take school pictures in the midst of an acne epidemic, Lunch Lady, Betty, and the Breakfast Bunch learn that Stefani is using them to break into the world of high fashion.
ISBN 978-0-375-87035-4 (trade pbk.) — ISBN 978-0-375-97035-1 (lib. bdg.)
1. Graphic novels. [1. Graphic novels. 2. School lunchrooms, cafeterias, etc.—Fiction. 3. Schools—Fiction. 4. Photographers—Fiction. 5. Fashion—Fiction. 6. Mystery and detective stories.] I. Title.
PZ7.7.K76Lup 2012
741.5'973—dc23
2011047994

The text of this book is set in Hedge Backwards.
The illustrations were created using ink on paper and digital coloring.

MANUFACTURED IN MALAYSIA
September 2012
10 9 8 7 6 5 4 3 2 1

First Edition